SHAPESHIFTERS

Tales from Ovid's *metamorphoses*

*This new transmogrification of Ovid's great and magical story-poem
is for my wife Celia, my children Alistair, Danny, Briony, Sasha and Beattie,
and for my grandchildren Arthur, Robin, Natasha, Charlotte,
Lola, Caitlin, Zoë, Annie and Lily,
with unchanging love – A.M.*

For Lillian, David, Elynor, Carmen, Kesella and Alice – A.L.

Shapeshifters copyright © Frances Lincoln Limited 2009
Text copyright © Adrian Mitchell 2009
Illustrations copyright © Alan Lee 2009

The right of Adrian Mitchell and Alan Lee to be identified as the author and illustrator respectively
of this work has been asserted by them in accordance with the Copyright,
Designs and Patents Act, 1988 (United Kingdom).

First published in Great Britain in 2009 and the USA in 2010 by
Frances Lincoln Children's Books, 4 Torriano Mews
Torriano Avenue, London NW5 2RZ
www.franceslincoln.com

Adrian Mitchell acknowledges the assistance of Arts Council England

LOTTERY FUNDED

British Library Cataloguing in Publication Data
available on request

ISBN: 978-1-84507-536-1

Illustrated with watercolours and Photoshop
Set in Berling LT Roman

Printed in China
1 3 5 7 9 8 6 4 2

SHAPESHIFTERS

Tales from Ovid's *metamorphoses*

RETOLD BY
ADRIAN MITCHELL

ILLUSTRATED BY
ALAN LEE

F

FRANCES LINCOLN
CHILDREN'S BOOKS

CONTENTS

INTRODUCTION

The clouds dance
to the split-second
finger-drumming
of the wind.

The mountain dances
to the deep beat
of century
after century.

Different tempos –
all one music.

If you want to watch shapeshifting, don't start with mountains. They do change, but they take their time. Much better to nip up in an airplane and look down at those famous shapeshifters, clouds. Clouds delight in forming themselves into unicorns, waterfalls, palaces, funny faces before your very eyes. They're great entertainers.

There are shapes shifting all round you. Evolution was the shapeshifting of blobs into reptiles into mammals into human beings. Our own Earth shapeshifted over the centuries from a fiery ball into a blue and green planet. Even now the continents are slowly moving under our feet and the universe is constantly altering its shape.

We're all shapeshifters. We change from eggs to foetuses to babies to toddlers to children to teenagers to parents to pensioners to dust. It's a strange kind of dance, but it has its moments.

Ovid loved the myths of Greece and Rome. In *Metamorphoses* he created a shining necklace of these stories. He brought them to life in a way which still seems fresh today. His stories are beautiful, funny and terrifying. They're full of happy and fatal surprises – and transformations.

As I studied these old stories, writing and rewriting them, I tried to change them so that they were more like themselves with every change. I attempted to make them clear-eyed, but never simple-minded. The stories didn't seem to me like the marble of a sculptor or a potter's clay. They were more like living creatures, alive and wriggling in my hands. I tried to hold them, but they kept changing – writhing, purring, snarling, scratching, snoozing, jumping out of my arms and escaping into the wild.

I'm sure my own beliefs have also sometimes influenced my treatment of the stories. So I'd better say what they are: like an elephant, I hate war and cruelty and value strength and gentleness. I take the side of the poor and helpless against the rich and powerful. I believe that the gods were made by human beings and not the other way round. And, like William Blake, I believe that everything that lives is holy.

Thank you, Ovid, for your beautiful poem.
Yours in admiration,

Adrian

peace

THE GREAT DANCE

Look at this world we're travelling on –
so beautiful and strange.
See the creatures all shifting their shapes –
everything has to change.

River and raven, mountain and man,
wombat and woman, trout and tree,
lofty and lowly – swiftly, slowly
they are all changing constantly.

Everyone and everything dances
to the music of changeability
and they shift their shapes as they swirl around –
yes, everything changes constantly.

Everything changes,
nothing stands still,
the dancers dance on
as they always will.
Child and animal,
flower and stone
dancing together,
dancing alone.

Though the dance-floor is rough
and the music is strange,
we laugh as we dance
to the music of change.

OUT OF CHAOS

Let's begin at the beginning:
Long before you or me,
there were no stars or sun or moon,
no sky, no land, no sea.

All that existed was chaos –
a mountain, broad and steep,
a universal rubbish dump,
an almighty compost heap.

Chaos – packed tight with tiny seeds and eggs
and squirming things, some with no legs,
some with no eyes, others with no head –
all tucked up in that massive bed.

Some were resigned to endless night,
some angry, looking for a fight
or burrowing to see if they were able
to find a way out of this Tower of Babel.

They were wrestling, nestling, scheming and dreaming
till one day the great heap started steaming,
for the ways of the gods and nature are strange
and they'd decided Chaos must change…

So something shifted,
something lifted,
something died and something grew,
something froze,
something rose,
something breathed and something blew.

The roots of the mountain
convulsed and quaked,
the whole cosmic pudding
simmered and baked.
The heap groaned – swelled – then in slow motion
all flew apart in a great explosion,
and suddenly – look, here's the ocean,
and up above it, the new sky
like a blue sheet hung out to dry,
and islands like cakes arranged on a tray,
some wooded and green, some rocky and grey.

Chaos has suddenly melted away
and look – here's the world on her first day!

And now, for the very first time, the sun
strides up the sky – our golden one.
He smiles down all morning and afternoon,
then bows to welcome his daughter the moon
as she walks in her dress of silver light
down the starry-clouded stairs of night.

The gods and goddesses made their home
in the regions above the Earth's blue dome.
They liked the new planet and great Jove said,
"That world should be inhabited."

They sent bright-shining fish to share the seas
with kindly porpoises and whales.
To rule the mountains and the trees
they made the eagles and nightingales.

Next, animals in every size and shape –
the speeding antelope, the busy ant,
the lumbering bear, the cheerful ape,
the drowsy dormouse and wise elephant.

Then they took handfuls of the new-made mud
to model the first man and the first woman.
They gave them limbs, nerves, brains and blood
and all the rest that goes to make a human.

And those two looked like gods, with heads held high
so they stood upright and could see the sky.
And that's how Chaos, once a formless face,
changed into Earth, home of the human race.

THE FOUR AGES

GOLD

The first age was the Golden Age.
Gold people always told the truth.
They had no laws, they had no king.
There were no judges and no prisons,
but these gentle, golden people
were not afraid of anything.

There were no clubs or swords or guns,
there were no soldiers or police,
but men, women and animals
lived in harmonious peace.

They didn't even have to plough –
Earth gave its vegetables free
and golden wheat for everyone,
the grape, the olive, the wild strawberry.

Cherry and apple trees grew wild,
walnuts to crunch and oranges to suck,
and blackberries like blue-black gems,
and acorns dropping on your head for luck.

Yes, it was always springtime then
and, in the cheerful April breeze
bright flowers dancing everywhere
like multi-coloured galaxies.

If you felt like honey, all you had to do
was find the tree where honeycombs hung,
lie on your back on the sun-warmed moss
and let the sweetness drip on to your tongue.

SILVER

Jove decided to rule the Earth –
he was bored and wanted something to do.
He made springtime shorter, to share the year
with winter, summer and autumn too.

For the first time the white-hot sun
blazed down from a merciless sky.
The first frost fell and the whole land
turned stony as the snow began to fly.

The good, gold folk who lived in caves
bright with paintings and golden laughter
were replaced by silver ones not as good,
but better than the bronze ones who came after.

These Silver Age people needed houses.
They had to plant acorns to grow an oak
and plough their fields laboriously
with bullocks under a heavy yoke.

BRONZE

Next, Jove tried a tribe he named the Bronze People,
always ready for a fight if you got on their wick,
and yet you couldn't call them really wicked –
simply bad-tempered and thick as a brick.

IRON

Last came the Iron Age. Hard times.
The world boiled over with evil crimes.
Out went kindness, truth and reason –
in came trickery, lies and treason.
Greed for money, greed for power –
the Iron Age was a poisonous flower.
(Did I say *was*? Is it safe to say
that the Iron Age has passed away?)

Rich men launch huge-sailed ships on the waves
before they know how the ocean behaves.
Graceful trees are hacked down and set afloat
in the shape of a clumsy, leaky boat
upon the unknown, dangerous sea.
The Earth, which belongs to everybody,
just like the sunlight or the air,
is measured out by a surveyor
and chopped up with walls and boundary lines,
fences, armed guards and Keep Out signs.

The greed of the Iron men never stops.
They strip the Earth bare of all her crops.
They dig and they tunnel down through the Earth's shell
to discover the wealth in the shadows of Hell
and drag it up shining into the light –
wealth Jove had hidden far from men's sight,
wealth that transforms a gentle man of prayer
into a homicidal slayer.

Now lethal iron bends to Man's will
and silver and gold, which are deadlier still.
Now War comes – crushing anyone who resists –
shaking iron and gold in his bloody fists.
War leaves no innocents alive –
only the cruel and cunning survive.

No guest is safe from his charming host
nor a friend from the friend who loves him most.
See the beloved sister and brother
spit and turn their backs on each other.
That husband's plotting to strangle his wife
while she poisons his soup to end his life.
Goodness is sick and likely to die –
so what are the gods doing up in the sky?

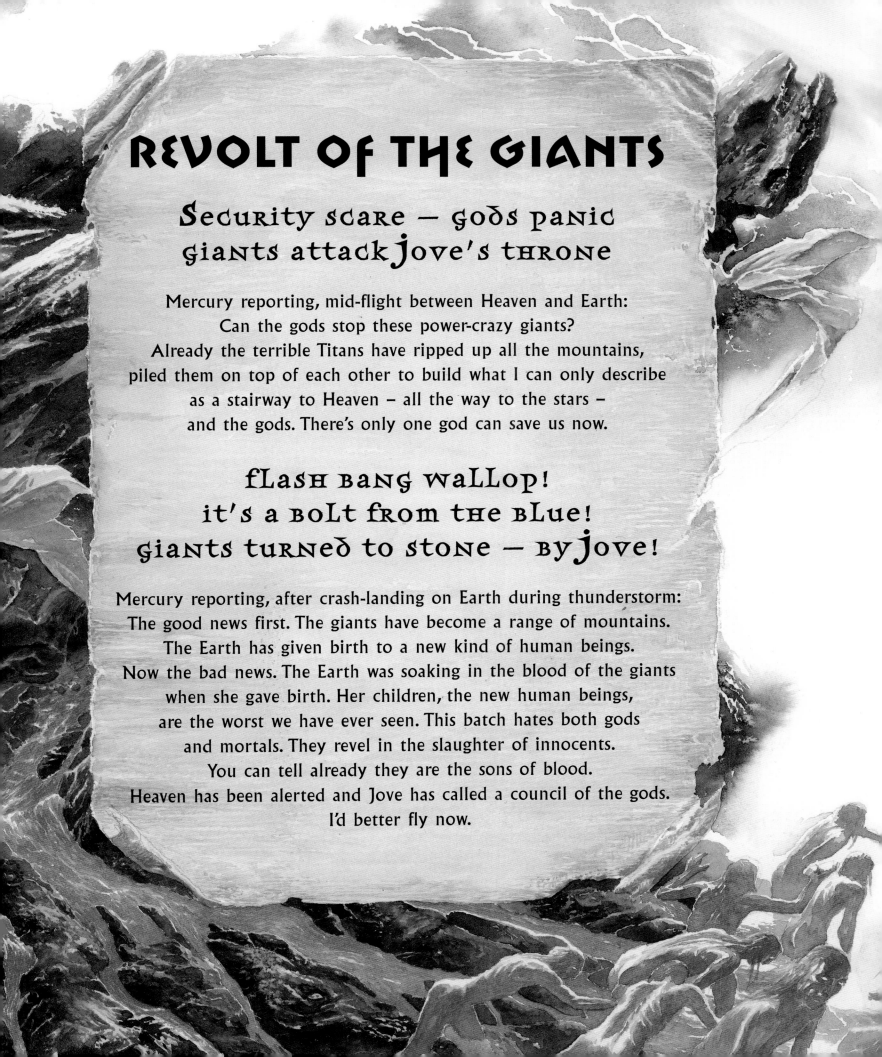

REVOLT OF THE GIANTS

Security scare — gods panic
giants attack Jove's throne

Mercury reporting, mid-flight between Heaven and Earth:
Can the gods stop these power-crazy giants?
Already the terrible Titans have ripped up all the mountains,
piled them on top of each other to build what I can only describe
as a stairway to Heaven — all the way to the stars —
and the gods. There's only one god can save us now.

Flash bang wallop!
it's a bolt from the blue!
giants turned to stone — by Jove!

Mercury reporting, after crash-landing on Earth during thunderstorm:
The good news first. The giants have become a range of mountains.
The Earth has given birth to a new kind of human beings.
Now the bad news. The Earth was soaking in the blood of the giants
when she gave birth. Her children, the new human beings,
are the worst we have ever seen. This batch hates both gods
and mortals. They revel in the slaughter of innocents.
You can tell already they are the sons of blood.
Heaven has been alerted and Jove has called a council of the gods.
I'd better fly now.

JOVE IN JUDGEMENT

Jove, watching from his high tower, gasped
at the cruel squalor of the human race.
He was consumed by an enormous anger
and called a council of the gods.

There is a road which runs along the heights of Heaven.
You can watch its traffic when the skies are clear –
we call it the Milky Way, famed for its shining whiteness.
Along this ivory highway the gods travelled
to the high halls of Jove, the mighty thunder-god.
Into this greatest of all palaces
all the lesser gods walked respectfully,
took their seats in the marble hall
and looked up to the throne expectantly.

Jove shook his dreadful locks three times,
stirring up the stars and oceans.
Then he spoke angrily:
"It was bad enough when those giants,
with snakes for feet and a hundred arms each,
tried to tear down Heaven and us along with it.
They were ferocious, but only one army –
I crushed them with a single fist.

"But now the Earth's full of our enemies.
They're nothing but bloodthirsty vampires.
I swear by the river of Hell that every mortal being
must be destroyed. You think I'm too harsh?
Let me tell you the story of just one of these human monsters."

THE WOLFMAN

Jove lowered his voice to a soft roar:
"Lycaon was his name – King of Arcadia.

"I'd heard stories of crimes all over the Earth,
too disgusting to be true.
Hoping to disprove them
I disguised myself as a human being
and went to see for myself.
The world was far worse than I thought.

"When I came to Arcadia, I gave a sign
that a god had arrived to visit the Earth.
The ordinary people began to worship me.
Then King Lycaon came out and laughed at them.
'I'll soon find out,' he said, 'if this is a man or an immortal.
I've got a very simple test.'
In his mind, which I could read, of course,
he planned to suffocate me in my sleep
with a smelly old pillow.
That was his very simple test.

"Not content with that
he took one of his prisoners,
slashed his throat open, boiled some of his flesh,
barbecued some other bits
and served them up on a golden dish.

"No sooner was that plate on the table
than I was on my feet.
I raised my avenging thunderbolt above my head.
I struck that house and brought it tumbling down.

"The king ran terrified into the fields,
then began howling, trying to speak.
He foamed at the mouth,
then, with his usual thirst for blood,
he charged a sheep, felled it and began
to tear it apart with his teeth and kept on tearing it
till it lay dead as mutton.
His robe began to change to shaggy hair,
both his arms twisted into crooked legs.
He became a wolf, and yet he kept
some traces of his former self.

"He had the same grey, greasy hair,
the same lopsided face,
the same bloodshot eyes.
Now his house has fallen,
but more than one house deserves to fall.
Let the whole human race be punished."

All the gods applauded.
The lesser gods applauded loudest.
The great gods were more thoughtful.
A few just nodded quietly.
Then doubts emerged – what would the world be like
if there were no human beings?
Who would be there to worship the gods?
Who would make sacrifices?
Who would tame the animals?
(And there was an unspoken feeling
that without being able to watch the mortals
act out their love affairs and wars,
immortal life wouldn't be so much fun.)

But Jove, of course, knew how they would think.
He promised them a new race of humans on Earth,
not like the first lot. The new ones would be marvellous.
Now he was ready to destroy the old gang.
He raised his thunderbolt. The gods held their breath.
Then he laid down the lightning – he had a better idea.
He would send down rains from every corner of the sky
and destroy humankind in one great flood.

THE GREAT FLOOD

Jove locked the north wind into a cave
with all the other winds which break up clouds.
But he unchained the southern wind
and let him fly out with soaking feathers,
beard heavy with rainwater,
and black clouds helmeting his head.

South wind grabbed the heavy, low-riding clouds
like a handful of dark brown sponges.
When he squashed and squeezed them with his hands,
a crashing sound circled round and round the Earth
and the full clouds poured down a deluge.
Iris, the goddess of the rainbow,
kept filling and refilling the clouds.

Wheatfields and cornfields were washed into mud.
But Jove was still angry with the wickedness of mortals.
He called on Neptune, his sea-god brother, for help.

Neptune called all the rivers of the world.
They flowed to his palace on the ocean bed.
He ordered, "Great rivers, now's the time to use your strength!
Overflow your banks, break down the dykes
and race each other to the sea."
Neptune struck the sand with his trident.
The world trembled and broke open.

Every buried spring leaped into the light.
Every dam strained, bulged and finally burst.
Waves like heaving hills of water
went storming over the land.
Roads became torrents, fields became foaming lakes.
Not only orchards, crops and herds of cattle,
not only men and women and children,
but sacred temples were swept away.
Any house or palace left standing
by the monstrous power of the waves,
was soon submerged, its roof far underwater,
its towers hidden deep beneath the flood.

There is no difference now between sea and land.
The world is all sea, a sea without a shore.

Here's a man who tried to run to the top of a hill.
The water ran faster than he could.
Here's another swirling round and round in a coracle
high above the field he used to plough.
He fainted from hunger yesterday.
He will not wake up again.
Here are two children perched high in an elm tree
chewing a salmon which got tangled in the branches.
How long can they last? Not long.
On the steep slopes where slim mountain goats once grazed
the sleek black seals are taking their ease.

Far below the waves water-nymphs
wander the streets
of underwater cities.
Sub-aquatic forests are invaded
by smiling dolphins
playing hide-and-seek among the branches,
shaking the apple trees as they pass.

On the surface, dog-tired wolves swim harmlessly
among panicking flocks of sheep,
lions and tigers are torn apart
by the ferocious waves.
The tough wild boar, the speedy stag
can't fight or outrun the massive deluge.
A wandering dove, which has searched
day and night for a place to alight,
finally falls, exhausted, into the everywhere sea.

Waves are smashing on the mountain peaks.
It seems that the world is drowned.

TWO SURVIVORS

There was no land left in the great ocean, only the two peaks of Mount Parnassus soaring up towards the stars. On the rocky slopes of this mountain a ramshackle raft came to rest. There were two exhausted old people on board, the only survivors of that terrible flood.

When they staggered ashore, the first thing they did was to offer thanks to the mountain's god, Apollo. They had lived good lives, Deucalion and his wife Pyrrha. But now they expected to be visited by death.

Jove looked down and saw the world was one enormous swamp. Many thousands had drowned, but one man and one woman were still alive, both innocent and good. So he tore the clouds apart and let them be swept away by the north wind. Suddenly the Earth could see the heavens again and the sky could see the land.

Neptune, great king of the sea, laid down his trident and calmed the waves. He called his trumpeter from the depths. Up came ocean-coloured Triton, his shoulders bumpy with barnacles. Neptune ordered him to blow his conch shell until it resounded round the world. Triton raised up his spiralling, twisted trumpet. His call was heard and understood by the seas and rivers. All of them returned to their proper places.

Once again the sea had shores. Rivers flowed within their banks. The floods fell back, the hills rose into view. The trees finally showed themselves, leaves still coated with slime. The world was itself again.

But Deucalion saw it was an empty, silent, desolate land, and he wept. He said to his wife, "My love, we're the only ones left. If only I had magic powers like my father, I could breathe life into moulded clay figures and repopulate the world. As it is, we two are the future of the human race. It must be the will of Heaven."

They wept together, then decided to ask the gods to help. They purified themselves by washing in the new river. Then they walked to the temple of Themis, goddess of justice. Its roof was covered with drying seaweed and the altar-fires were dead.

The couple threw themselves down on the ground, kissing the shrine's damp stone steps and calling out for help. Themis pitied them and said, "Walk away from my temple. Veil your faces. Loosen your robes. And throw behind you your mother's bones."

The two of them stood there, amazed, unable to move. Then Pyrrha stammered, "Great goddess, forgive me, but I couldn't outrage my mother's ghost by treating her bones like that." Silence. They repeated the words of Themis to each other, trying to understand.

Finally Deucalion had an idea. "Either I'm going mad or – no – the goddess would never tell us to commit a crime. Perhaps she means the Earth's our mother. And the bones of the Earth must be the stones – I hope." They looked at each other; it could do no harm to try.

So they veiled themselves and loosened their clothes and filled the folds of their robes with stones. Then, as they walked, they threw the stones, one by one, over their shoulders.

These stones – and this is historically true – began to lose their hardness. Gradually they softened and almost melted into new shapes. As the stones grew and became gentler in nature, they began to take on a rough likeness to the human form. The likeness wasn't exact – more like half-finished marble statues, with rough outlines and corners.

Those parts which were earthy and dampish changed into flesh. The solid and rigid parts became bones. The veins in the marble became veins for blood to pass along. And soon, as Heaven willed it, the stones the man had thrown were changed to men, the stones the woman threw took on the shapes of women. This is why we are so hard, this is why we can endure so much: we are children of the stones.

WRONG ARROWS

After the great flood, the Earth grew fruitful in the sun and gave birth to every species of animal. Some creatures were the old ones restored to life, but some were new and weird as witchcraft.

One of these was a new and gigantic snake, the Python, who terrorised the newly-created race of men. Apollo, god of the bow and arrow, had never killed anything except deer and wild goats. But now he loosed a thousand arrows, almost emptying his quiver, until the Python's poisonous blood gushed from his deep black wounds.

To make sure this deed would never be forgotten, Apollo founded the sacred Pythian Games. At these games, every winner at boxing, running or chariot-racing was honoured with an oaken garland.

The first woman Apollo fell in love with was Daphne, daughter of the river-god Peneus. This was all the fault of spiteful Cupid. The trouble started when Cupid was bending his bow and Apollo made fun of him:

"Hey, little boy, that's a man's weapon! Let me take it. I've got the strength to strike down a wild beast and the skill to hit him smack in the heart. I killed the Python with more arrows than you could count. He swelled up and burst, and his dark blood covered the land. Stick to tickling lovers with your little darts, and stop imagining that boys can go to war."

Cupid answered back: "Apollo, your bow may conquer all the animals, but mine will conquer you. As a muddy human is to a glorious god, so are you to me."

The boy-god shook his wings and soared up through the blue air to land on the shady peak of Mount Parnassus. There he chose two arrows which have opposite effects. One of them lights the flames of love, the other puts them out. The one which rouses love is made of gold and has a sharp, shining point. The other arrow is blunt and tipped with lead.

Cupid shot the leaden arrow into the heart of Daphne. But with the other he shot Apollo. So Apollo burned with love – but Daphne, revolted by the thought of him, ran far away to hide in the forests.

Many would-be lovers looked for her – but she cared for none of them or for marriage, and spent her days roaming the trackless woods. Her father often said things like, "Daughter, give me a son-in-law," or, "I'd really like a little grandson."

But now Daphne believed all love was horrible. She blushed and clung to her father and said, "I want to be single for ever and ever."

Apollo sees her, loves her and wants her for his bride. He burns like a forest fire. He looks at her disordered hair and longs to comb it for her. He sees her starry eyes and perfect lips, but gazing is never enough. He wonders at her fingers, her hands, her wrists and her arms, bare to the shoulders. He believes that what is hidden must be even lovelier.

Daphne runs away from him faster than the wind. She doesn't falter when he shouts after her, "Daphne, please stop. I'm not your enemy. Stop! That's how a lamb runs away from a wolf. But I don't want to devour you, I want to love you. Don't run so fast – you'll fall and tear your lovely skin on the brambles. Slow down and stop.

"I'll slow down, too. I'm not some scruffy goat-herd. If you knew who I am, you wouldn't run away. Jove himself is my father. I have the power to tell all that has been, all that is and all that will be. I'm the one who invented harmony with my songs and my lyre-playing.

"I am an archer and my aim is true. Oh, but one arrow, even truer than my own, has pierced my heart. You know, I discovered the art of medicine. They call me the healer – but I can't cure this love of mine or heal its hurting."

He would have said more, but Daphne ran on. How beautifully she ran! But the hunt could not last for ever, for the young god decided to save his breath for running. Just like a hound who spots a hare sit up in an open field and gives chase with flying feet, and, gaining on her, grazes her heels as she bounds ahead, not sure if she is doomed or not – that's how he hunted her.

He ran with hope, she ran with fear – but he was faster. Now her strength was fading quickly. Pale with terror and collapsing, she reached her father's river and touched its water, crying out, "Father, help me! Let your sacred river change me! Wash away my fatal beauty."

At that moment a dragging numbness coursed through her arms and legs. Her soft body was wrapped in thin, smooth bark. Her hair became leaves, her arms were turned to branches. Her feet, which were so swift only moments ago, put down deep roots. Her lovely head was now the green crown of a tree. Only Daphne's shining loveliness remained.

But still Apollo loved her. He placed his hand on the tree's trunk and felt her heart still fluttering under the bark. He stroked the branches as if they were a woman's arms and kissed the tree again and again. Even the bark of the tree shrank away from his lips.

Apollo cried out, "You can never be my bride, but you shall always be my tree. My golden hair, my lyre and my arrows shall always be entwined with your leaves of laurel. Victorious Roman generals shall wear laurel wreaths. Laurel trees shall stand on either side of the palace door as trusty guardians. And, just as my head is forever young and my hair is never cut, so you will always keep the beauty of your leaves."

He had said all he could say. The laurel tree waved her newly-created branches and seemed to move her crown in full consent.

THE BLACK CLOUD

There's a rocky waterfall in Thessaly
showing rainbows in its spray,
and a pretty young woman called Io
goes strolling near the falls one day.

Well, the great god Jove sees Io
and begins his honey talking:
"Sweet girl, step into this shady wood
for the sun's too hot to walk in.

"If you're scared of wolves or lions
I will shield you from all harm,
for I'm the god of the thunderbolt –
don't run, girl! Take my arm!"

But she's gone! Jove scratches his mighty head.
How can he cure her fear?
"I'll disguise myself as a harmless cloud –
what an inspired idea!

"For a cloud can change to any old shape
which is useful when you're wooing;
wispy and white or heavy and black –
depending what it's doing."

The weather report says, "Cloudy,"
when Io walks out next day.
Then a huge black cloud comes swooping down
and envelops his pretty prey.

Jove's wife Juno, looking down,
wonders why the sun's gone dim.
She looks around Heaven for her husband –
not a sign of him.

Juno thinks, "He's up to his tricks –
that cloud's just another disguise…"
So she glides down and blows away the cloud
and there the great Jove lies.

But Jove hears Juno coming
and transmogrifies Io – POW!
He changes the girl to a snow-white heifer,
still lovely, but just a cow.

"Nice bit of beef," says Juno.
"What do you call that breed?"
"I call it Io," says the god.
"I grew her from a seed."

"Wonderful, darling," says Juno.
"Well, I think she's delicious.
She can be my pet." – Jove has to agree
or his wife will be suspicious.

So the goddess leads the heifer
away as her helpless prize
and for safety's sake puts her in the care
of Argus of the Hundred Eyes.

Yes, one hundred eyes around his head,
all keeping a sharp look-out,
(though two at a time take a restful nap,
turn and turn about).

Wherever he stands he can watch her,
even behind his back.
He allows her to graze on sunny days,
ties her up when the sky turns black.

She munches bitter herbs and lies
on the stony ground to dream.
She drinks the chilly water
from a muddy little stream.

She wants to appeal to Argus –
is there nothing he can do?
But all of her eloquent speeches
come out as a plaintive moo.

She stares at her own reflection
down by the waterside,
but a head with a muzzle and horns stares back
and she runs off, terrified.

Her loving father passes by
without a second look
till she follows him and blocks his path
beside a little brook.

How can she tell him who she is?
How will he ever know?
Then she raises one hoof and writes in the mud
the letters I and O.

He looks in her huge, brown toffee eyes
and his tears begin to flow.
He throws his arms round her velvet neck
and cries, "My sweet Io!"

Argus the bodyguard struts up
and pulls the pair apart,
then drags Io to a distant field
to graze with a broken heart.

But Jove is angry. He calls up
his son, swift Mercury:
"Fly down to Earth, my shining one –
kill that bug-eyed Argus for me."

Mercury dons winged sandals,
grabs his hypnotic wand
and leaps into space as easily
as a boy dives in a pond.

He changes himself to a herdsman
driving goats past the cascade.
Argus calls, "Join me on this rock –
it's cooler in the shade."

Mercury joins him and plays his pipes –
soporific lullabies
which close down seventy, eighty-six,
but never all hundred eyes.

For Argus fights to keep awake
though he is fascinated.
"What are these pipes you play upon,
and how were they created?"

PAN PIPING

Mercury smiles, and tells this tale:
"On the mountains of Arcady,
there lived a nymph called Syrinx,
lovely as a silver tree.

"The woodland satyrs and mountain gods
loved Syrinx desperately.
She escaped them all by speed and skill
and kept her virginity.

"But one day Pan, god of the woods
begged her to be his bride.
She ran fast as light, but his hairy arms
caught her by the riverside.

"She cried, 'Transform me, water-nymphs,
kind spirits of this place!'
And Pan found a bunch of hollow reeds
locked in his hot embrace.

"He sighed his sadness, and those sighs
passed down the reeds a tone
which sang so soft and sorrowfully
it would melt a heart of stone.

"Said Pan, 'Sweet wood-nymph, this is how
I'll whisper love to you.'
So the pipes were joined together with wax
and called Pan-pipes. That's true."

Now the hundred eyelids of Argus
flicker and close in sleep.
Mercury makes a pass with his magic wand
to ensure his trance is deep.

And he draws the hooked sword from its sheath
and he swings it high in the air
and he slashes down across the neck,
just below the greasy hair,

And the head hurtles over the waterfall,
streaking the rocks with blood.
Argus is dead, his hundred eyes
lie blind in the river's mud.

Juno rescues those eyes and sets them with gems
in her favourite peacock's tail,
then, in her jealous anger,
sends a Fury on Io's trail.

This fiend hunts the heifer around the world
with terrors sharp and vile,
and finally leaves her cowering
on the banks of the river Nile.

That night Io throws back her head
and stares up at the galaxies,
and her plaintive mooing seems to say,
"Gods, end my suffering, please."

Jove puts his arms round Juno:
"Let Io's agony end,
for I swear that she shall never give
offence to you again."

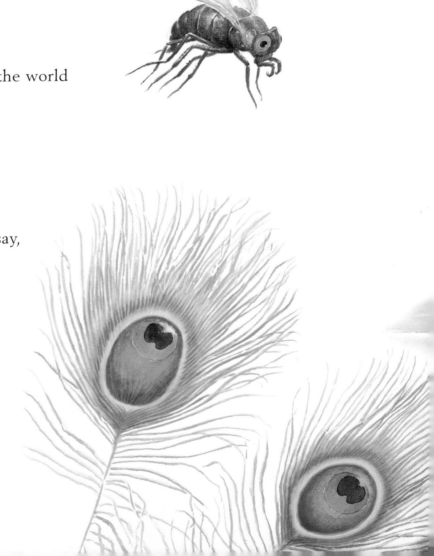

Juno's anger melts away.
So does the heifer's fear
as Io changes back to a nymph –
her horns and hoofs disappear.

And those big brown eyes grow smaller
and the rough hair falls away
and the nymph stands on two feet again,
beautiful as the day.

Io's life isn't quite the same.
One thing is hard to do:
she's nervous if she has to speak
for fear that she might moo.

But Io is a goddess now,
she's worshipped far and wide.
She has a son who looks like Jove
and he stays close by her side.

Her son's name is Epaphus
and he always keeps an eye
on those ever-changing, shifting clouds
floating across the sky.

CHARIOT OF FIRE

Talking of Io's son Epaphus, there was just one thing in the world he couldn't stand – his brother Phaethon. Phaethon was always boasting about being the son of the king of the gods – until one day Epaphus exploded and told him Jove wasn't his father.

Phaethon, a hot-headed young man, ran to his mother Io and demanded to know, "Who's my real father?" Io was angry too. She held her arms up to Heaven and looked straight at the sun.

"Your father's Apollo, the sun-god himself. If I'm not telling the truth, may I never see the light again. If you don't believe me, go and ask the Sun."

Joyfully Phaethon jumped into the air and began to fly across Ethiopia, the ocean and the lands of India, to the place where the sun rises.

And there it stood, rising high on lofty columns, bright with fiery gold and bronze. The roof was gleaming ivory, the tall doors polished silver. The Palace of the Sun.

Io's son climbed the steep path to the palace, and looked upwards. He stopped, too dazzled to move. There sat Phoebus Apollo, god of the sun, on his emerald throne. To his right and left stood the Hours and Days and Months and Years and Centuries.

From his throne, the Sun, whose eyes see everything, read the mind of the nervous young man and said, "Phaethon – you are my son, and one any father would be proud to acknowledge."

The young man answered, "Great Apollo – Father, if you let me use that name, prove it to me. I want everyone to know I'm your son."

His father put aside his blazing crown of light and beckoned to the lad. Then he embraced him. "Of course you're my son. Io told the truth. Ask me for anything – anything at all. I swear by the River Styx you shall have it."

Right away the lad asked for the loan of his father's golden chariot and the right to drive his winged horses for one whole day.

Four times Apollo shook his shining head. "I wish I could take back my promise. But I can't refuse you now. Please ask for something else.

"Listen – it's far too dangerous. You're too young and not strong enough. The gods themselves wouldn't dare ride my chariot of fire. Even Jove himself, who hurls the thunderbolts, couldn't control it – and nobody's greater than Jove.

"The road's impossible. The first part is steep. My horses, for all their early morning freshness, can hardly climb it. When I get to the top of the road, way up in the middle of the sky, the seas and land are so far below that even I am too scared to look down.

"Next the descent – a sheer drop. That's when you need incredible strength to hang on to those horses. What's more, the heavens and the stars are spinning in the opposite direction to your journey, whirling and making you dizzy.

"Could you face the spinning poles of the Earth and not be spiralled off into space by their force? Maybe you think the skies are full of golden orchards, holy cities and temples full of treasure?

"No, the road is plagued by ferocious beasts. Even if you manage to keep on course, you must pass the sharp horns of the Bull, and confront the Archer and the jaws of the angry Lion. Up there the Scorpion's claws stretch out to clutch you and the Crab looms over you.

"And you can't control my fire-breathing horses if they rebel against their reins. My son, look around the beautiful world and ask for anything – it's yours. Don't ask me for this fatal gift."

But Phaethon threw his arms around his father's neck. "Please let me drive the chariot, father."

Apollo had sworn an oath, so he led his son to the chariot, which was made by Vulcan the blacksmith-god himself. Its axle and shaft were gold. The wheels had spokes of silver. Jewels glowed and glittered all over the harness. It was a great work of art.

Now the stars had set and the morning star, last of all, had left his watch-tower in the sky. The sky began to redden. It was dawn.

Apollo ordered the Hours to harness his horses and they quickly did so, leading them from their stables breathing fire and filled with a breakfast of ambrosia.

Apollo anointed his son's face with flame-proof ointment and placed on his head the shining crown of the sun. He sighed as he gave these final warnings: "Spare the lash, lad, and hold tight to the reins. Don't try to gallop straight through the five zones of Heaven. Your best way runs slantways, avoiding the southern skies and the far north as well.

"Drive through the middle of the air. If you fly too high, you will burn the skies. Fly too low and you burn the Earth. Hold your course midway between the Serpent and the Altar.

"Now it is dawn, the day must rise. Take the reins! Or take my advice instead." But the young man had already mounted the chariot and stood there proudly, taking the reins joyfully and thanking his father.

The Sun's four horses – Blazes, Daybreak, Flame and Fireball – stamped and whinnied impatiently. The gates opened. Out dashed the horses, tore through the clouds and swooped upwards on their beating wings.

But the horses of the Sun noticed something strange. The chariot was much lighter than usual. Just as ships with too little ballast roll in the waves because they're too light, so the chariot, without the weight of a god inside it, bounced along on the bumpy air.

Feeling this, the team ran wild and veered off their usual road. Phaethon panicked. How could he handle such heavy reins? Where had the road gone? Even if he could find it, how could he control these galloping brutes?

His knees shook with fear, his stomach clenched and his eyes went black with vertigo. Suddenly he wished he'd never taken his father's horses, wished he hadn't discovered who his father was. The chariot swept along like a ship with a broken rudder at the mercy of a hurricane.

What can he do? He's travelled almost halfway up the sky, but even more of this dizzying highway lies ahead. He hangs on to the reins, he tries to shout orders, but he can't remember the names of the horses.

A monster looms up in front of him – the Scorpion, stinking of black poisonous sweat, swings its curving tail at him and he sees the vile sting. Hiding his eyes with his hands, he drops the reins.

When the horses feel the reins flopping on their backs, they run wild. Out they thunder into the unexplored regions of the sky. They stampede, crashing against stars, climbing to the peak of Heaven, plunging down headfirst, nearer and nearer to the Earth. The moon is amazed to see her brother's horses flying below her own, and the cloudbanks begin to smoulder in the heat.

And now the Earth bursts into flame. The highlands burn first, and their rocks split into deep cracks and their lakes hiss and become clouds of steam. The meadows are burned to white ashes. All the trees are flaming torches. There are greater losses. Great walled cities die, whole nations are burned to death. All the famous mountains burn, from the Alps to the Caucasus.

Now Phaethon sees the whole world on fire. He can't bear the enormous heat. Each breath he takes feels like swallowing a furnace. The chariot floor is white-hot under his feet. The air around him is full of ashes and swirling sparks and thick, hot smoke. He can't see his desperate hands in front of his face.

The Earth breaks into great cracks, and light, penetrating to the Underworld, terrifies the king and queen of the land of the dead. The great ocean shrinks in the heat. Dolphins dare not leap above the sea. Three times Neptune tries to lift his head and shoulders out of the water – three times he submerges, unable to withstand the fiery air.

Though she is burning alive, the Earth heaves up her face and cries to the king of the gods, "Jove, if I've deserved all this, please let me die quickly by your lightning-bolts. Is this my reward for all my generosity to humans, beasts and gods?

"Even if I deserve to die, what has the sea ever done? At least have pity on the heavens themselves. Look around you: the heavens are burning. Soon the palaces of the gods will collapse. If the earth, the sea and the sky all die, we'll be hurled back into chaos. Save whatever is left to save."

Jove rises up into the heights
of Heaven. He has no clouds to spread
across the Earth, he has no rains to send down
through the sky. But he thunders and, balancing
the lightning in his right hand, flings it from beside his ear
at Phaethon, hurling him out of the chariot and out of life.

The crazed horses leap apart, breaking away from their reins.
The wreck of that great chariot is scattered all across the heavens.

But Phaethon, his hair in flames, is hurled headlong and falls, leaving
a long trail through the air. It seems like the moment when a star in the
clear heavens, although it does not fall, seems to fall for ever. The water-
nymphs find his body, still smoking with the flames of that thunderbolt.
They bury it, and carve this epitaph upon his tomb:

HERE LIES PHAETHON, A CHARIOTEER WHO FELL.
HIS FALL WAS GREAT, HIS COURAGE GREAT AS WELL.

His father, sick with sorrow, hides his face away; and so, for one
whole day, there is no sun. There is only the light of the burning Earth.
But Phaethon's mother Io wanders the whole world. At last she finds his
bones, buried in a foreign land. She weeps beside the tomb and her three
daughters join her there in useless laments for the young man.

After four months of mourning, the oldest daughter complains that her
feet are icy cold. When the second daughter comes to help her, she is
clamped to the ground by wooden roots. Their younger sister, trying to
tear her own hair, grabs at nothing but leaves. Now their ankles are
surrounded by bark, their arms extend into long branches. As they watch
helplessly, the bark closes round their hips, their waists, breasts, shoulders
and hands. Only their lips are left, calling out for their mother.

She tries to tear the bark from their bodies. Twigs snap off in her hands.
But blood flows from the white wood. Each daughter cries out, "Spare me,
mother. Goodbye now – " and the bark seals off her last words.

The tears of these three weeping willows continue to flow. They are hardened into amber by the sun. They drop from the tree and are carried down the river, to be made into necklaces worn by brides in Rome.

King Cycnus, Phaethon's best friend, abandons his kingdom to mourn beside the same river. As he cries aloud, his voice becomes higher and higher. White feathers hide his hair and his neck stretches longer and longer. His reddened fingers are webbed together, a black lump appears on his forehead and his mouth turns to a blunt beak.

So Cycnus becomes a strange new bird – the first swan. He never trusts the upper air or Jove, because he remembers the fiery thunderbolt which killed his friend. Hating fire so much, he chooses to haunt quiet pools and lakes and so do all his children, to this day.

Apollo the sun-god sits eclipsed in mourning, hating himself and the light of day. "That's enough," he says, "No more travelling for me. Let somebody else drive the chariot. If none of the gods can do it, let Jove be the charioteer. He'll soon find out that the lad who failed to control those fiery horses didn't deserve to die."

All the gods gather anxiously around Apollo. They beg him humbly not to leave the world in the dark. Jove explains why his thunderbolt had to be thrown. Finally he orders Apollo to drive the chariot. Jove is all-powerful. So the sun-god harnesses up his team again, and whips them into action, screaming angrily at the terrified horses, "You killed my son!"

TRANSITION

The world, once drowned in a great flood
and left as an empty patch of mud
has soon, thanks to the sun and rain
and the kind gods, grown green again.

And now great Jove makes an intense
inspection of Heaven's battlements
in case the firestorm has caused subsidence.

Once satisfied, Jove turns his mind
to Earth, the home of humankind.
He heals the ocean, shore to shore.
The blackened forests flower once more.

The gods arrange and rearrange
this world which is so new and strange –
the only constant thing is change.

So many magic transformations,
mutations, transmogrifications,
shapeshifting, translations – all of these
are what I call metamorphoses.

So many changes through the ages –
to tell them all would take ten million pages.
After the last long tale I thought I ought
to tell you two which are very short.

BEARS IN SPACE

After the great fire of Phaethon, Jove was wandering the battered world one day. He was supposed to be repairing it, but his attention was diverted from ecology to biology. Jove himself caught fire when he saw a nymph called Callisto.

Callisto was beautiful and dangerous. She chased wild animals with a spear and birds with a bow and arrows. Diana the Huntress looked kindly on nymphs like that. But goddesses do not look kindly for very long.

Callisto was resting in a forest glade on a warm and sleepy afternoon. Jove saw her lying there, eating honey, all alone. "My wife's far away in Heaven," he said to himself. "She'll never find out. Even if she does, it's worth it." (In this lofty manner do the gods meditate.)

Swiftly he assumed the alert face and graceful body of Diana, goddess of the moon. He said, in his best Diana voice, "Sweet girl, most loved of all my followers, where have you been hunting?"

Callisto stood up. "Greetings, goddess. You are far greater than Jove himself. I'd say that even if he could hear me." Jove laughed, delighted to be prized more highly than himself. He kissed her on the lips.

She tried to tell him about her day's hunting, but he stopped her speech with a hot and overwhelming embrace. Callisto, nobody's fool, realised that she was not in the arms of the virgin goddess. She struggled, but the almighty Jove conquered her, said a quick goodbye and flew home to Heaven.

Some time later, the real Diana came walking through the woods with her virgin followers. At first Callisto hid – in case this was Jove in disguise again. But Diana called her to join her sisters.

The nymphs realised from Callisto's blushes what had happened. Diana invited her to join them swimming in a pool. But the young woman was reluctant. When Diana ordered her to undress, the reason was obvious – Callisto was pregnant. "Go away!" said Diana. "You shall not pollute my sacred pool." (For only virgins may enjoy the company of the Huntress.)

Juno, the wife of Jove, knew about her husband's spell of female impersonation. She waited until Callisto had given birth to a boy, Arcas. Then she took her revenge. "You'll pay for this!" she shouted at Callisto. "I'll take away your precious beauty, little huntress!"

She caught the young woman by the hair and threw her face down on the earth. As Callisto stretched out her arms to beg for mercy, they became rough with shaggy black hair. Her hands changed to feet tipped with sharp claws. Her lips, which Jove had kissed so recently, became broad, ugly jaws, and her words calling for mercy altered to a low growling.

But she kept her human feelings. She showed her grief, stretching her paws to the heavens, remembering the ingratitude of Jove. Often she was driven over rocky hills by the baying of hounds, the huntress hunted. Although she was a bear, she shuddered at the sight of other bears on the mountains. She was even afraid of the wolves, though her own father, Lycaon the Wolfman, ran with the pack.

When Arcas was fifteen, he still didn't know what had happened to his mother. One day he was hunting in the woods. Suddenly he found himself face to face with a she-bear. The bear stared at Arcas. It seemed as if she knew him. He shrank away from those huge brown eyes. He was terrified but didn't know why. When she lumbered up to him, whimpering, Arcas raised his spear to pierce her breast.

But almighty Jove held his arm back. He caught both mother and son up in a whirlwind and set them in the heavens where they became neighbouring stars. We call them the Great Bear and the Little Bear.

Remember those two bears in space whenever you eat honey.

INFORMER'S PAY

There's nothing the gods seem to enjoy more than a visit to Earth. They like to put on a disguise and trick some nymph or woman into making love. (You and I might be more inclined to use godlike powers to get into rock concerts or football matches, or even to rob banks – but all the gods seem to think about is love, love, love.)

One day Apollo chose a cowherd's rough cloak, a wooden staff and a set of Pan pipes and went wandering through the meadows. While he was tootling seductively on the pipes and dreaming of love, his cattle drifted away into a neighbouring field.

Mercury spotted them – an excellent herd – and hid them in the woods nearby. Nobody saw this theft except an old man called Battus. He had three teeth and was meant to be looking after a rich man's horses.

Mercury took him by the shoulder and said, "Look, if anybody asks you if you've seen any cattle round here, you haven't seen so much as a cowpat, all right? Do that for me, and you can have this spare cow." And the god of thieves pointed to a fine heifer, which the old man accepted with a gummy grin.

Battus pointed to a granite rock and said, "Your secret's safe with me. That rock will talk before I will." Then Mercury pretended to go home. But he changed himself into a rich, fat man in purple robes and waddled up to Battus.

"I say, old boy, give us a hand. Have you seen a herd of prime cattle round here? They're missing, presumed stolen. Come on, spill the beans and I'll give you a healthy cow and a bull to go with her."

Battus fell for it. "They're right over there, in the woods."

And so they were. Mercury dropped his disguise and laughed aloud.

"You old villain – you've betrayed me to myself!" He raised his silver wand and the old man was turned into a rock. Today this is the famous Touchstone Rock. Lovers still touch it and vow eternal love.

And, as lovers do, they always keep their promises.

THE HUNTER HUNTED

It was sheer bad luck. It's not a crime to lose your way on a mountain. But there may be a terrible punishment.

They'd been up since early morning, hunting in the woods on the mountainside. Now it was noon. A hot sun stared down at the young men. The keenest huntsman of them all, young Actaeon, was happy. "Enough killing for today, lads," he said. "We've done well. At dawn we'll start again. Let's go home, rest a little – and then feast a lot."

They packed up their gear and the pheasants, rabbits and deer they'd killed and started for home. Actaeon took a short cut, scrambling down between rocks. But he found himself in a valley he'd never seen before, among towering pines and graceful cypress trees.

He was standing, though he didn't know it, in the valley of Gargaphie. This is a green place sacred to Diana, virgin queen of the moon and goddess of hunting. Hidden away in the most secret part of the valley is a shady cavern, shaped like a rocky archway. A clear spring bubbles from the cave, becoming a silver stream and then a deep pool surrounded by mossy banks. Here the goddess of the wild woods, tired after hunting, likes to bathe in the bright water.

Yes, it was very bad luck for Actaeon. Shortly before he arrived in the valley, Diana herself walked into the cave with her nymphs. One took her spear and arrows to be cleaned. Another caught the queen's robe as she slipped it off her shoulders. Two more untied her silver sandals.

Her favourite handmaiden braided those wild-flowing locks. Then Diana dived from a rock. She swam and floated and smiled as she lay in her favourite pool. She was happily naked, like all her nymphs. She mounted the rock and prepared to dive again.

Suddenly there was a snapping of branches, and a young man – the lost Actaeon – walked heavily over the moss, stopped – and stared.

Blasphemy! He had no right to gaze on the goddess, especially when she was naked. The nymphs cried out and crowded round Diana, trying to hide her shining body. But she was taller than the rest of them.

Diana's face blushed like the dawn. She would gladly have shot this intruder but her bow and arrows were out of reach. So she dived and swam underwater towards the blasphemer. She surfaced, took a handful of sacred water and hurled it in the young man's face. As she drenched his hair, she told him, "Now you're free to tell the world you saw Diana naked – if you can find the words."

That's all she said – but from his head sprouted the high antlers of a stag. His neck stretched itself out. The tips of his ears folded into points. His arms became long legs and his body was soon bound tightly in a dappled, hairy hide.

He turned and galloped away from Diana, amazed that he could travel so fast. He saw the reflection of his muzzle and antlers in the pool and tried to cry for help. But no words came, only groaning snorts. Tears ran darkly down his furry cheeks. Only his mind was unaltered.

What could he do? He was too ashamed to go home to his family, too afraid to stay in these dangerous woods. He discovered a grove of trees where he could hide. Darkness fell and he tried to sleep. But his dreams were full of blood and terror.

Actaeon woke at dawn. He levered himself up on to his four legs and tried to think. But his mind felt strange. Away in the distance, he spotted a pack of hounds snuffling along – his own hounds. Then they saw him:

A long-legged deerhound called Blackfoot appears,
halts by a tree-stump and pricks up his ears.
He's joined by the keen-scented Thundercloud –
sniffing the pathway and baying aloud.
Down through the trees pour the rest of the pack –
Actaeon's hounds upon Actaeon's track.

Greedy from Crete is the dog in the lead,
then Graceful from Sparta – and then a stampede –
Rockeater, Deerslayer and Redclaws,
Hunterboy, Harpywing, Openjaws.
Dangerous gallops with Woodsman and Sure
and Glen, who was gored by the tusk of a boar.

There's Shep, who was raised by a wolf in the wild,
and Catcher's two puppy-dogs Bitter and Mild.
There goes skinny Sprinter, there's Gnasher and Spot
and Tigress and Mighty and good old Jogtrot.
Next come Tornado and low-running Swallow,
as Mellow and Bellow and Cypriot follow
with whiteheaded Fury and Grabber and Flame
and Barker and then – too many to name
(though Vandal and Vampire are present today
with Mudlark and Murder and Castaway).

The powerful pack,
thirsty for blood,
pours down the track
like a howling flood.

The stag's antlers turn
as he looks back.
He shouts, "I'm Actaeon!
You're my pack!"

But no words come –
only a sigh.
The baying of hounds
fills the whole sky.

Shadow is first
in the attack,
jabbing his fangs
in the deep-furred back,

then Deadly jumps up
from the rear
and every tooth
is like a spear,

and Vaulter leaps down
from a boulder,
clamping his jaws
in the stag's shoulder.

These three started last
but they got there first.
They hold the stag
and do their worst.

And now the whole
of the pack is here,
over and under
and round the deer.
There is nothing but tearing
and pain and fear.

A groaning is heard
by a huntsman nearby,
but how could it be
a human cry?

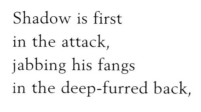

Now the stag's on his knees
as if in prayer,
and he turns his great head
and sees, standing there

his old hunting friends
shouting gladly, "Halloo!"
to urge on the hounds
as they always do.

And they look around, calling out
Actaeon's name.
"You'll be late for the kill!
That'd be a shame!"

But Actaeon's deep
in a huntsman's hell –
wishing he'd not trained
his hounds so well.

The last that he hears
are his friends' happy cries.
Then the agony's over -
the stag-man dies.

The moment Actaeon died, the anger
of Diana the huntress vanished and she forgot all
about him. Some of the gods thought she had been too cruel.
Others said she was firm but fair. Both sides put excellent arguments
to support their points of view.

SEX CHANGING

Jove was drinking nectar with Juno
and joking, as great gods do,
"I'll bet women have more fun making love
than poor males ever do."

Juno, she took the wager.
She told him there and then,
"Sometimes it's fine for women,
but it always works for men."

They called the wise man Tiresias
up to the heavens above.
But I'd better tell you how Tiresias
knew both sides of love.

One day he was out in the forest
when he saw two mating snakes.
He hit them apart with his walking stick –
then suddenly got the shakes

and he changed from a man to a woman,
and she spent seven years that way
till she saw those same snakes making love
in the middle of the forest one day.

She said, "I hit you once before
and you transmogrified me.
So I'll hit you again, you magical worms,
and we'll see what we shall see."

So she hit the wriggling serpents
and shivered in her changing skin.
She fell to the ground, but when he stood up
he was definitely masculine.

So Tiresias knew about gender –
he'd studied it from either side.
He didn't want to argue with gods
but they forced him to decide.

"A woman gets more pleasure
than a man, that's what I find."
Juno lost her bet and her temper too –
she struck Tiresias blind.

Jove tried to compensate him
for the fact he couldn't see
with the gift of seeing the future –
the power of prophecy.

KISS THE MIRROR

Soon the whole world discovered that the blind Tiresias, who had been both a man and a woman, always told the truth about the future. And many people came to ask advice, for everybody thinks they want to know the truth, until they hear it.

The first person to seek him out was the water-nymph Liriope. She had given birth, in her own river, to a beautiful son called Narcissus. Liriope carried him to the prophet and asked, "Will he have a long life?" Tiresias answered, "He will, if he never meets himself."

For a long time the words of the sightless seer made no sense. But what happened later proved them true.

Narcissus was sixteen – you could call him a boy, you could call him a man. Many young men and women were attracted to him. But the slim Narcissus was cold and proud. Nobody could touch his heart.

One day, after a deer hunt, he heard a nymph call out to him. Her name was Echo – at this time she still had a body as well as a voice. Echo could never keep quiet when others spoke. But she was never the first to speak.

This was because Echo had acted as a look-out for Jove when he was making love to nymphs on the mountainside. When Juno, Jove's jealous wife, found out, she punished Echo. "You've tricked me once too often," she screamed. "Now I'll twist your wicked little tongue. From today you will only be able to repeat what others say – and only for a moment."

"Meant," replied Echo, and could say no more. When Juno laughed and laughed, Echo could only answer, "Ha!"

After that, she could only repeat the last phrases of any voice she heard.

Echo was sitting up in a tree, watching the songbirds teach their young to fly. Glancing down, she saw the handsome Narcissus wandering down a green path. Her light heart burst into little flames. She wanted to go to him and whisper words of love in his ear. But she could only wait for him to say something she could answer.

Narcissus was looking for his friends. "Anyone here?" he called, and Echo answered, "Here!" Astonished, he stared around him, and called out again, "Hey, can't you see me?" and she called down, "See me!"

He looked back, saw nobody and cried, "Why do you run away from me?" And was answered with the one word, "Me?" He stood still, bamboozled by that voice. "Come over here and join me!" he shouted. Echo, who had never repeated sounds more happily, called, "Join me!"

She decided to put these warm words into action. Leaping lightly from her tree, she ran to him and tried to fling her arms around his neck. But he dodged and ran, shouting back at her, "Keep your hands off me! I'd rather die than surrender!" All she could answer was, "Surrender!" – nothing more.

Rejected and ashamed, she left her tree and went to live in a lonely cave. But her love didn't fade away – it grew heavy with grief. She wept so much that she cried away all the moisture in her body. Her skin shrivelled and flaked away. Then only her bones and voice were left. Her bones turned to stone and only her voice remained, only her voice was still alive.

That's how Narcissus rejected her. He turned down many others too – mountain-nymphs, water-nymphs, mortals – he laughed at all of them. Finally, one spurned young man prayed to Nemesis, the goddess who punishes the proud: "May he fall in love as deeply as I did, and never win his love!" The goddess heard his prayer and smiled her cruel smile.

In the woods lay a peaceful pool. It had been there for hundreds of years. It was clear and bright, with a silvery surface. Nobody knew how deep it was. No shepherds ever came there, or goats or cattle. No bird or animal or falling bough ever disturbed its perfect stillness. Tall grass grew round it and trees bent inwards to shade its waters from the sun.

One hot day, Narcissus broke through the undergrowth and saw the pool for the first time. The pool was beautiful: the young man was thirsty. He crouched down, made his hands into a drinking bowl, and drank. But as he drank, he was astonished by the sight of a most beautiful creature.

He was suddenly in love – in love with a shimmering glassy shadow – but he believed his own reflection was real. Spellbound, he stared down at himself. He lay there gazing at his twin, lay still as a marble statue. He gazed down into his eyes, those twin stars. He examined the riotous curling locks of his hair, worthy of Bacchus or Apollo. He viewed, as in a vision, his smooth cheeks, his ivory neck and the fine features of his face.

Without understanding what was happening, he longed for himself. A hundred times he kissed the water. He plunged his arms into the pool, trying to clasp the neck he saw below. He didn't know what he was looking at, but he knew he wanted it desperately.

What a fool – he might as well try to hug a shadow. All he had to do was turn away, and his loved one would vanish. He came with you, Narcissus, he stays with you, and he will go with you – if you can ever bring yourself to go!

Look at Narcissus: nothing can draw him away from the bank of the pool. Stretched out on the shady grass he gazes and gazes down into his liquid mirror. There he sees his love: a pink image at dawn, a golden image by day, a fiery image at sunset, a dark image at nightfall, a silver image by the light of the moon.

He stands up like an actor, opens his arms to an audience of trees and declares, "Wise woods, was there ever a crueller love than mine? You'd know – you have always been a hiding-place for lovers. You've stood and watched them for hundreds of years. In that time, can you remember one lover who suffered as terribly as me? That face enchants me. I look into those eyes and they stare back. But I can't touch that face or kiss those eyes.

"Worse than that – the two of us aren't parted by a mighty ocean, or a long and dusty road, or a mountain range, or locked city gates. Only a little water keeps us apart. He is eager for my embrace. Whenever I offer my lips to the shining pool, he lifts his lips to mine. He *must* care – so little separates our loving hearts.

64

"Come up through the water to me, whoever you are! Why do you slip through my fingers? Surely I'm young and good-looking enough for you. All the nymphs fall in love with me.

"The way you look at me gives me hope. And when I stretch my arms towards you, you stretch yours towards me. When I smile, you smile back. When I cry, I've often seen tears upon your cheeks. When I nod my head, you nod, and I'm sure, from the way your sweet lips move, you answer my words as well, with your own silent words of water."

Slowly Narcissus sat down on the bank. Gradually he realised. He raised his hands to cover his mouth, then whispered, "Oh, he is me! The image in the pool is me. I'm in love with myself. What shall I do? I can't woo myself. What I long for, I have already. I wish I could fly out of my body.

"But now my sadness drains away my strength. I must die a young man's death. Death will end all my troubles. I wish my beloved could outlive me – but we two have to die together."

He looked down again into the bright pool, at his own image. His tears caused ripples, blurring the picture of him in the waters. As he saw it melting, he cried out, "Where are you swimming away to? Stay here! Let me look at you, even though I can't touch you."

In his agony, he tore at the top of his tunic and beat his bare breast with white fists. Where he struck his chest, the skin began to glow – like apples, partly white and partly red, or unripe grapes hanging in clusters whose skins appear to blush.

The pool was still again. Now he could see himself and bear no more the pain of love. As yellow wax melts before a gentle fire, as the frost melts in early morning sunshine, he gradually dissolved in his own hidden fire. He had no colour now. He had no feelings, no mind, no beauty any more – not even the body Echo loved so much,

Echo saw him dying and she pitied him. Each time he moaned aloud an "Oh!" she answered with an "Oh!" His last words, as he gazed into the pool, were these: "Poor boy, so dearly and so hopelessly loved," and she repeated, "Loved".

And when he said, "Farewell!", "Farewell!" was Echo's answer. Narcissus lowered his tired head into the green grass, and those two shining eyes which loved their master's beauty so intensely – they grew dim, and their lids were closed by death.

When old Tiresias was told about the tragedy, he said, "What a shame he had to meet himself."

Even when he entered the Underworld, Narcissus kept on gazing at his reflection in the River Styx. The water-nymphs and wood-nymphs mourned him, and Echo repeated their laments. They prepared a funeral pyre for him. With flaming torches they searched for Narcissus – but no body could be found. Where it had lain, they found a single slim flower – white petals round a golden centre. We call it the narcissus.

THE BOY GOD

Sometimes the world chugs along from day to day
doing the same old things the same old way.
Then suddenly a new god arrives in town
turning everyone inside-out and upside-down.

That's how it was when Bacchus appeared
out of the blue, all belly and beard,
with his drunken singing of liberty –
free wine, free love – oh, everything free
as he rode in his panther-drawn Bacchusmobile
with a wild pack of women and men at his heel
all boozing and bawling wild songs against war
and work and virginity – things Rome stands for!
The men we relied on to fight foreign powers
spent their strength upon poems and battles of flowers.

This new god said, "Do what you want to do! Right?
Do you want to party all day and all night?"
And the people screamed, "Party!" and shook their maracas
and banged on their drums as they drank to great Bacchus.

Now, there are thousands of stories about Bacchus, but most of them
are very doubtful. Since the god lives his life as one long party, there are
seldom witnesses who can remember exactly what happened on this
beach in the Adriatic or that valley in Sicily. They start the story, then
rub their heads, mutter – and reach for another drink.
   But I was told this story by an honest fisherman, name of Acoetes:

My father was a fisherman.
He never read a book
but he taught me how to steer a boat
and how to bait a hook.

My father died one stormy night
and when they read his will
all that he had left me was
his boat and a fisherman's skill.

I hired a crew in a wine shop
and sailed out to the west
and we stopped one night at an island
to get some food and rest.

I sent my men for water
from a nearby mountain stream,
but when they came back, they were dragging
a boy out of a dream.

He seemed to stagger like a man
sleepwalking, full of wine,
but from his beauty I could tell
his nature was divine.

'The boy's a god,' I told my crew,
then turned to the lad to say,
'Whoever you are, please bless us all
and pardon us today.'

'He's just a kid from Naxos
and we're kidding him,' said the crew.
'We'll sell him into slavery
and get a fine price, too.'

'I'll take no part in that,' said I,
for I hate slavery,
'but I'll steer this boat for Naxos –
if that's where he wants to be.'

They knocked me down, they beat me up,
they lashed me to the prow.
When I said, 'Better set me free,'
they said, 'We're the masters now.'

But they veered off to the north-east
and the young god turned around:
'You promised to take me westward
to Naxos' holy ground.

Why are you taking me away?
What have I ever done?
Where's the courage in kidnapping –
so many against one?'

They mocked the boy as they rowed on,
that powerful, cruel crew.
(Let me remind you that each word
of this brief song is true.)

For suddenly the ship stands still
as if in a dry dock.
The crew tries to row twice as fast,
the ship stands still as rock.

Then ivy creeps along the oars,
winding and binding them down,
and spirals swiftly up the mast,
over the sails and round,

twisting all over the ship with vines,
hanging in clumps of green.
And now, with garlands of glowing grapes,
Bacchus himself is seen.

He is no boy. He's a bearded god.
Tigers lie at his feet.
He laughs and holds his spear aloft.
Panthers surround his seat.

The crew are maddened by the sight
of the god guffawing there.
They leap into the ocean
but are all changed – in mid-air.

Their bodies blacken,
their backbones bend,
their noses hook,
their jaws extend.

Their skins are hardened,
shining scales.
Their arms are fins,
their feet are tails.

All round the boat
the creatures leap,
up through the air,
down to the deep.

Like dancing girls
they sport and play,
breathing in water,
snorting out spray.

Twenty-one men went to sea,
only one man survives –
the rest are twenty dolphins
leading dolphin lives.

Bacchus turns to me and says,
'That's how the story ends.
Now, sail me home to Naxos,
live with me and my friends.'

If you don't believe this song of mine,
come to Naxos any night.
Join me and my mate Bacchus
in a Bacchanalian rite.

THE BRIDE OF DARKNESS

Who was the first to plough a field?
Who was the first to milk a cow?
Who was the first to pass good laws?
Who was the first to grow wheat and corn?

Lovely Ceres was the first,
goddess of harvest festival.
Give thanks to green and golden Ceres
every time you eat and drink.

There was once a violent giant called Typhon who tried to storm the gates of Heaven. The angry gods hurled him down into the blue ocean. They heaped his struggling body with earth and rocks and boulders. Today we call this heap the great island of Sicily.

Typhon lies, growling, on his back. The volcano of Etna weighs down his head. Often he vomits up smoke and flames. Or he summons up all his strength and tries to push the stones and the cities off his body. Then the Earth quakes, and cracks apart.

King Dis, ruler of the silent Underworld, was disturbed by these eruptions. What would happen if the Earth's crust burst open? The glare and hubbub of the world would flood down into his land. His subjects, most of them sensitive ghosts and shades, would be scared out of their wits.

Dis, drawn in his ebony chariot by four black horses, rode up from his gloomy kingdom to inspect the foundations of Sicily. "Seems safe enough," he murmured to himself. "Seems satisfactory." His dark grey face almost smiled the shadow of a smile.

Venus, the adventurous goddess of love, saw Dis standing there. He was the loneliest of gods. None of the goddesses would marry him – it would mean living in his grim, twilight palace far underground.

Venus hugged her son Cupid and told him, "Quick, shoot your arrow into the heart of that dismal god. You and I rule the gods of the Earth and Sea. Why not conquer the Underworld as well? Let's make Dis fall in love with Persephone, the daughter of Ceres. Otherwise she'll stay a virgin for ever, like those stubborn ice-goddesses, Diana and Minerva."

Cupid chose the sharpest of his thousand arrows, fitted it to his bow, drew it back and shot it right through the dark heart of Dis.

Not far away lies a deep pool, populated by tall white swans and their grey cygnets. Trees gather round the pool and cast cool shadows on its banks. Bright coloured flowers of every kind grow there in an everlasting springtime.

Persephone was playing with her friends. They were decorating their hair and dresses with flowers – violets and lilies of the valley. Persephone shone with happiness.

All in one moment, Dis saw her, fell in love with her, grabbed her up in his strong arms and carried her off in his black chariot. The terrified girl called for her mother Ceres. The goddess heard her and ran to help. But she followed the echoes of her daughter's screams, not the screams themselves, up into the mountains.

The dark chariot was rumbling downhill. The top of Persephone's dress was torn. Small flowers spilled out. The girl was such an innocent that she wept for the loss of a few violets. Her kidnapper urged on his horses, shouting out their names and snapping the dark reins against their necks. "Midnight! Black Flame! Deadlight! No Name! Faster!" They galloped through pools of boiling sulphur and past the battlements of Syracuse.

From the waters of her lake rose the water-nymph Cyane. She saw her friend Persephone being stolen away. "Stop!" she cried. "If you want to marry the girl, you have to court her." And she stretched out her arms, trying to block the path of the chariot.

But Dis, son of Saturn, boiled over with anger. He whirled his double-fanged royal sceptre in his hand, then hurled it into the water. The rocky bed of the lake cracked, opening a steep road to the Underworld. Down plunged the chariot into the land of the dead.

Cyane's heart was broken. She wept and wept and melted into the waters of her lake. You could see her arms and legs softening, her bones beginning to bend, her nails floating away and vanishing. Her hair, her face and her body too, all of her beauty melted away into the cool waters. And last of all, her living heart dissolved and there was nothing left but the silent waters of the lake.

Ceres, terrified, searched for her lost daughter all over the world. By day she hunted for her child under the merciless sun. When night fell she tore up two pine-trees, set them alight in the crater of Mount Etna, and carried them as torches through the frosty darkness.

She was staggering with weariness and thirst. Then she saw a small hut thatched with straw. She knocked on the door, and out came an old woman, who stared at the goddess.

When Ceres asked for a drink, the old woman gave her sweet barley water. As she drank it gratefully, a rude little boy watched her. He laughed and called her greedy. Ceres, insulted, threw the rest of the drink, complete with barley grains – splat! – in his face.

Right away his cheeks exploded with spots, his arms were squashed and bent into legs and he sprouted a long tail. He shrank and shrank until he was smaller than a lizard. The old woman, amazed and sobbing, bent down to touch this little miracle, but it zipped away into a hole in the wall. Some people call him the star-spangled newt.

After Ceres had searched every country and ocean, she came back to the lake of Cyane. The nymph longed to tell her where her friend had been taken, but now she was all water, so she had no words. She could only rescue from the bed of the lake Persephone's favourite scarf, lost when the chariot dived, and let it float up to the surface.

Ceres knew the scarf, of course. She cried and shook her fists, but she still didn't know where her daughter had gone. She shouted angrily at the whole world, calling it an ungrateful place which didn't deserve her gift of harvests. She laid a special curse on Sicily, where she had found the scarf. She broke up ploughs with her bare hands. She cursed farmers and their cattle too, she ordered the fields not to bear crops and blighted the corn seeds as they lay sleeping in their sacks.

The fields of Sicily, famous for their fertility, withered. Corn burned in the relentless heat. Then the rains came, and the crops drowned. Icy winds raged. Greedy birds snatched any seeds that were sown. Tough grass and thistles strangled the surviving wheat.

Finally the water-nymph Arethusa raised her head from her green pool, shook back her dripping locks and spoke to Ceres:

"Kind mother, who has filled the world with crops and fruit, please don't be angry with a land which has been true to you. Sicily is innocent. It was invaded by the thief who stole your daughter.

"When I was swimming in the underground river called the Styx, I saw your Persephone with my own eyes. Her face was sad and fearful, and yet she is now a queen, the great queen of darkness, the wife of Dis, tyrant of the Underworld."

Ceres stood as if turned to stone. At first she couldn't even think, let alone speak in words. A great pain rose from her heart and she stepped into her chariot and drove upwards to the lands of Heaven. There she appeared, hair tousled from her flight, and spoke indignantly to Jove:

"I'm here to plead for my daughter and yours – Persephone. If you don't care about me, at least take pity on her. My daughter disappeared, but now she's been found, and it seems she's lost for ever. Make Dis bring her back – a kidnapper's not the right husband for our sweet daughter."

Jove answered, "Persephone is our daughter. This may be a crime, but it's a crime of passion. If you give your consent, kind goddess, Dis will not disgrace us as a son-in-law. After all, he's my brother. But if you're determined to separate them, Persephone may walk in the open air again – but only if she has eaten nothing in the Underworld. That's the decision of the Fates. No appeal."

Now, Persephone had been fasting in the lands of the dead. But as she walked through the twilight orchards of the Underworld, she picked a pomegranate from a bending bough and, peeling off its yellow rind, ate seven seeds.

Nobody saw this but a spiteful boy, who ran and told King Dis. So the new queen of the shadowlands could not return to Earth. Enraged, she changed the informer into an unlucky bird. She threw in his face a handful of water from the fiery river Styx. Suddenly he grew an ugly beak, feathers and bulging eyes. He sprouted yellow wings and long, hook-shaped talons. He grew fat as a pig, too lazy to move a feather. He became that most disgusting bird, that bringer of bad luck, the lurking screech-owl.

Then great Jove, to do justice to both his lonely brother Dis and his sad sister Ceres, divided the earthly year into two parts. Now Persephone spends the warmer, brighter months with her mother on the Earth, and the colder, darker months with her husband in the Underworld.

Until this judgement, Persephone had only shown a sad face to Dis, but now happiness came back into her heart. Dis thought that the sun, hidden so long by dark and wintry skies, had scattered the clouds and shown its face – Persephone smiled.

And even now, when the snows begin to melt and the dark purple clouds of winter fly away and crocuses shine in the new grass and lambs wait in their mothers to be born – Persephone returns to Earth, carrying the springtime in her arms.

She stays with us all through the summertime, but when the leaves of the forest turn yellow, brown, red and golden, when the first leaf falls, Persephone kisses her mother and then, smiling, walks down the secret passage to the Underworld. And there she reigns as queen, all through our wintertime.

THE YOUNG CRITIC

Pirithous, who's a teenage clown
swigged a bottle of my best wine down
and then he made a speech like this
with lots of drunken emphasis:

"I've listened to your fairy-tales for hours.
I tell you, gods don't have the powers
to change man into mouse or dog into cat
and every this into a that."

Everyone gasped – but he kept blathering,
"And even if they can mutate one thing
into another by shapeshifting –
the business of making these transformations,
substitutions, quick-change alterations,
whole body transplant operations,
switches, shuffles, transmogrifications,
atom-swapping and grasshopperations
amounts to no less than a frivolous way
for gods to act – that's what I say."

I stared at him, my face bright red.
  "All right, young man, we heard what you said.
    That's enough, shift your shape up to bed!"
      (At breakfast next day that young critic so wild
        appeared in the shape of a hungover child.)

HOSPITALITY REPAID

Don't underestimate the powers of Heaven.
The gods can do whatever they like – I can prove it.
Way up in the hills of Phrygia,
overlooked by a broad-shouldered mountain,
an oak and lime tree grow side by side,
surrounded by a little stone wall
and guarded by a gander and a goose.
Not far from the trees lies a dark swamp
for comic ducks and one tall priest of a heron.

Jove came here once, disguised as a man,
with his son Mercury, minus his winged sandals.
They walked from house to house
like travellers in search of a warm bed.
They knocked upon a hundred doors,
a hundred doors were slammed in their faces.
Only one house welcomed them in –
a ramshackle cottage thatched with straw
and reeds from the swamp.

When Philemon was a young man
and Baucis a young woman
they were married in this cottage.
They lived and grew old together
in the same quiet place.
They carried the burden of poverty lightly,
for they were contented and not ashamed.
There were no masters or servants in their house –
only the two old lovers.

So, when two gods came visiting,
stooping under the low doorway,
Philemon fetched a bench
and Baucis covered it with a bright counterpane,
inviting the visitors to sit and rest.
The goose and gander at the fireside
neither hissed nor spat at the visitors,
but stood and lowered their beaks in homage.

Baucis raked the cooling ashes in the hearth
and brought the embers back to life,
feeding them with leaves and bark,
blowing them till they glowed and flamed
with breath from her old lungs.
Then, on the fire, she placed a copper pan of water.
Philemon cut a cabbage
from the well-watered garden
and chopped off the outer leaves.

The old man took a long forked stick
and hoisted down a side of smoky bacon
which hung from a blackened beam.
He cut a thick slice of this precious meat
and lowered it into the bubbling water.
While this was cooking, the couple entertained
their visitors with stories.

They smoothed a mattress of soft grasses and moss
over a couch of willow-wood,
and this they covered
with their best sheets and blankets, worn but clean.
Any stranger, beggar, exile or king,
should be offered the best of everything.
The gods reclined upon the couch.

The old woman, with shaking hands,
tried to lay the wobbling table –
one of the table-legs was short,
so she propped it up with a broken cup.
Now the table was level,
so she wiped it down
with a handful of green mint.
Then she brought a wooden plate
of green and black olives,
Minerva's favourite fruit.

Next, autumn cherries steeped in wine,
endives, radishes, creamy cheese and eggs
baked carefully in the warm ashes –
all these in small dishes of earthenware.
Then a wine-bowl of rough pottery
and goblets carved from beechwood.

Cabbage and bacon soup was enjoyed by the gods
and good red wine as well.
For the next course – nuts, figs and shining dates,
plums and sweet-smelling apples in small baskets,
purple grapes fresh off the vines
and at the centre of the feast
a honeycomb, glowing white and golden.
And all round the table
goodwill, warmth
and lively, happy faces.

Then the old couple were amazed
to see the empty wine-bowl shake itself,
and fill again, wine welling up from nowhere.
They were scared. Their guests were gods.
They knelt and offered up a timid prayer
asking forgiveness for such a humble meal.

Baucis and Philemon had only two animals.
They were Marcus and Hesperi,
a goose and gander who liked to stand guard
over their little kingdom.
They ran to catch and roast them
for their distinguished guests.
But the geese had wings which were swift and strong,
the old people were lame and slow.
Time and again Marcus and Hesperi dodged them,
then they flew and tried to hide
under the gowns of the gods.

Jove smiled and said, "Don't kill the geese.
We are gods in disguise.
The mean-minded people round here shall be punished
for their rudeness to us.
But you two shall be spared.
Leave your cottage and come with us
to watch from the mountain-top."

The old people obeyed.
Leaning on their staffs
they struggled upwards over stony ground.
One arrowshot from the peak
they turned around.
The entire landscape below was flooded.
Only their house remained above water.
As they stared in amazement
and wept for their drowned neighbours,
before their very eyes they saw their cottage
transformed into a temple.
Marble columns replaced its wooden frame.
The thatch turned yellow and became
a roof of shining gold.
They saw rich carvings on the doors
and a mosaic pavement of many colours
in their front garden.

Jove asked them gently, "Good people,
what is your dearest wish?"
The two consulted, then the old man said,
"Do you think we could possibly be your priests
and guard this temple for you?
And, because we've always been together,
allow us both to die at the same time,
so I never have to see her tomb
and she never has to bury me."

Their wish was granted.
As long as they lived
they looked after the temple.
Marcus and Hesperi guarded it well.

Finally, one summer evening,
when they were withered by old age,
they stood talking of old times
in front of the holy temple.
And as they talked
Baucis noticed little leaves growing
all along Philemon's arms
and he saw she was sprouting leaves as well,
and as the foliage grew over their faces,
while they were still able to speak,
they both whispered the same words,
"Goodbye, my love –"
just as the bark closed over their lips.

And even today the local peasants
point out those two trees hugging each other
as they grow from one double trunk.
Together… together…
together for ever.
I was told this story by old men
who had no reason to tell me lies.
I visited the place myself and saw
a flock of geese fly over to the swamp.
There were good luck tokens on those two trees
and I added my own wreath of wild flowers,
because I think we should remember those who are loved by the gods,
and I know we should love all those who have loved so well.

QUICK-CHANGE ARTIST

There are some great heroes
whose shape is changed once
and they stay that way for ever and always.
There are other heroes
who have the power
to change their shapes as often as they like.

Proteus is the most famous
of the second kind of shapeshifter –
for he's a one-man everything.
One moment he looks like an ordinary young man,
the next, he's a snarling lion.
The lion vanishes and
now he's a wild boar charging
with blood-stained tusks.
The boar twists round – it has become
a serpent poised to strike.
Sometimes he hardens into a stone,
and often stretches up into a tree,
now he melts into flowing water
and he's a mighty river.
Now he's a flame, the enemy of water.

Don't get in a fight with Proteus.

THE KING OF HUNGER

That reminds me of a young woman named Mestra.
She was given the same powers as Proteus
and found them useful, as you shall see.

Her father was a man who scorned the gods
and never offered them any sacrifice.
His name was Erysichthon,
but he became known as the king of hunger.

One day he picked up an axe of steel,
marched to the sacred grove of the goddess Ceres
and started to chop down the ancient trees.

Among them stood the holiest tree of all,
a giant oak, centuries old,
decorated with wreaths of flowers
placed there in thanks for prayers granted.

Often the wood-nymphs danced around
the trunk of this great oak,
circling hand in hand
under its generous shade.

That mighty trunk was thirty metres round
and towered over other trees
as ordinary trees tower above the grass.
But even so, this king ordered his slaves
to cut down the sacred oak.
They all were afraid to touch it, so
the king raised his own axe and shouted,

"Even if this is the tree that Ceres loves,
even if this tree is the goddess herself –
today its leafy top shall crash
down to the ground."

He raised his axe to deal a slanting cut.
The oak of Ceres trembled and groaned,
its acorns and leaves turned pale
and all its branches became white.

The axe struck. From the wounded trunk
blood seeped – then poured from the hurt bark.
Now it was like a great white bull,
his throat cut for a sacrifice.

The slaves stood terrified, but one of them
tried to hold back the royal axe.
The king glanced at the man and said,
"Take this payment for your piety –"

and turned his axe away from the tree
and chopped off the man's head.
Then he turned back to the oak
and struck blow after blow after blow.

From inside the tree a deep voice spoke:
"I am a spirit beloved by Ceres.
I live in this oak and I prophesy
gladly that you will be punished soon."

But the king and his intimidated slaves
completed their murder of the tree.
Weakened by countless wounds, dragged down by ropes,
the tree staggered and fell heavily,
shaking the earth, shattering many lesser trees.
All the wood-nymphs were broken-hearted.
In robes of black they went to Ceres,
goddess of farming and the harvest,
and begged her to punish Erysichthon.

The lovely goddess agreed
with a nod of her golden head,
and the wheatfields and cornfields, heavy with grain,
trembled as they do in the icy north wind.

She decided to punish the wretch with hunger.
But Ceres and Hunger may never meet,
so she sent for one of the mountain-nymphs
and spoke to her like this:

"There is a frozen land called Scythia
where no crops grow and no trees flourish,
for the earth is one enormous rock.

"In that gloomy iceberg of a land
live shuddering Cold and screaming Terror
and Hunger, the queen of famine.

"Go and ask Hunger to climb down into
the stomach of that tree-murderer,
and whatever the villain eats
let Hunger never be satisfied.

"Don't be frightened by this long, hard journey.
Take my chariot drawn by dragons –
they'll fly you through the air."

The nymph found herself staring down
from her borrowed chariot
upon the granite mountain-top called Caucasus.
There she landed and hitched the dragons
where they could drink from a fountain of fire.
She started looking for Hunger.
She found her in a field of stone,
tearing with fingernails and teeth
at skinny weeds and thistles.

Hunger's hair hung down in greasy knots,
her eyes lay deep and dim
like two stale redcurrants
sunk in her bloodless face.

Her cracked lips stank of vomit.
Flakes of scurf covered her neck and throat.
The skin of her belly was so dry and thin
you could see her twitching, empty entrails.

Her scrawny hip-bones stuck out like knives.
Below her hollow loins
her withered breasts swung dismally
from her crooked spine.

Her arms and legs had wasted away to sticks
but their joints were massively swollen
so her elbows and knees and ankles appeared
like swollen balls of yellow ivory.

The nymph came as near her as she dared
and delivered the goddess's commands.
Though she kept her distance, she could feel
the freezing breath of Hunger.

Then she summoned the dragons
who cowered behind the chariot,
hitched them up, geed them up, drove steeply into the sky
and over the seas to Thessaly.

Hunger and Ceres are opposites,
but Hunger obeyed her orders –
she swam through the air on the waves of the wind
until she reached the palace of the king.

It was the middle of the night.
The king was sleeping deeply
as Hunger crept into his room
and took him in her bony arms.

She breathed into his nose and mouth,
filling him full of her contagious breath,
his throat and lungs and bloodstream –
soon they were all awash with hunger.

Her mission completed, she left the fruitful world
and flew to her home
in the lands of Nothing.

Gentle sleep, hovering on silent wings,
still soothes the dreaming king.
What is he dreaming of?
Feasting.

He chews his own saliva greedily,
he grinds his teeth against each other,
he cheats himself by gobbling and swallowing
imaginary food.

For all his dream banquet
of roast meat and game,
rare fishes and exotic fruits
is nothing more than air.

The king wakes up. His jaws ache
for food and his stomach's burning.
He calls out for every kind of food –
everything land, sea and air can provide.

The palace tables are loaded with delicacies
and he wolfs them all down and calls for more food.
He cries out, "I'm still hungry,
fetch me more! Yes, and more!"

It's enough to feed a city.
It's enough to feed a country.
It's enough to feed the world –
but it's not enough for this one man.

The more he stuffs himself,
the more he wants.
As an ocean welcomes every river
yet never overflows,

as a bonfire never refuses wood
but can burn more logs than you can count
and will burn a whole forest
and still roar for wood,

so the hands of the king
grab all the food within reach
and cram it down to his belly.
But the more he eats, the emptier he feels.

Now he has spent all his riches on food,
but Hunger isn't tired of the game
and his greed rages on.
Finally all his treasure has been sold

and he has next to nothing left.
But not quite nothing.
There is still his only daughter, Mestra.
(She deserves a better father.)

He sells Mestra down at the slave-market
to buy himself more food.
But Mestra's spirited, she won't be a slave.
She runs down to the sea, home of the god Neptune.

She stretches her hands out over the waves
and cries, "Save me from slavery –
you who stole my virginity."
(Neptune had taken it while she was bathing.)

The sea-god grants her wish.
He waves his trident and changes her
into a brown-faced fisherman with rod and net,
a rough coat and boots like fishermen wear.

The man who bought the lovely Mestra
stares at this rugged fellow and says,
"Hey, you, I can see you're a skilful angler
by the way you dangle the worm on your hook.

"I hope the sea will stay calm for you
and the fish trust you and take your bait."
The fisherman Mestra looks straight through him
and, "Thanks, mate," she says in a gruff voice.

He tries again. "Where's she gone?
Where's the girl who was standing here just now
with the wild hair? She was standing where you are
and her footprints don't go any further."

She sees that Neptune's gift is working.
Glad to be asked about herself, she says,
"What girl? Sorry, mister,
I've been concentrating on the fish.

"I swear by the fisherman's god Neptune
that for a long time now
no man has stood upon this shore
except me, and no woman neither."

Her legal owner believes every word.
He nods, and turns, and leaves her on the sand.
After he's out of sight, Neptune appears
and restores Mestra to her proper shape.

That's not the end. Her father finds
that Mestra has the power to change her form at will.
And so he sells her again and again
to many masters.

But each time she escapes again
as a mare, a dove, a deer, away she goes
and is sold again, thus raising the money
to feed her insatiable father.

But in the end, when he has eaten everything
King Erysichthon, hungrier than ever,
begins to feed on his own body,
tearing his arms and legs with his teeth,

twisting himself into grotesque shapes
so he can chew up as much of the flesh
as his mouth can reach, till finally,
still hungry, he eats himself to death.

ORPHEUS SINGS

The wedding started badly. Hymen, the god of weddings, did attend, but he gave no blessings and smiled no smiles. The lucky torch he held sputtered all through the ceremony, filling everyone's eyes with smoke and tears.

The bridegroom was Orpheus, son of Apollo and the greatest singer and musician in the world. His bride was the beautiful, vivacious Eurydice. It should have been a great wedding. It was a tragedy.

As the bride danced in the meadows with her friends the water-nymphs, a snake bit her ankle and its venom killed her. Orpheus mourned her, singing desperately and playing the lyre with all his heart.

Finally he decided to go and look for her down in Hades. He climbed down through the cave of Taenarus to the Underworld. There he walked among crowds of ghosts and wraiths, until he found Persephone seated beside the ruler of that ugly kingdom, Dis, lord of the dead.

Orpheus played his lyre and sang:

> Rulers of the Underworld,
> all mortals bow down to you.
> I bring no lies or flattery
> but sing you what is true.
>
> I haven't come here to steal Cerberus,
> that three-headed dog at your side.
> I've come down here because a snake
> has killed my lovely bride.
>
> I've tried to live without her,
> but dark are the lands above.
> I was forced to come and seek her here
> by the famous power of love.

Now you may not sing about love down here
but I think you know it well.
If the story of Dis and Persephone is true
then love reigns here in Hell.
By all the terrors of the Underworld,
by this vast and silent territory –
please reverse the fate of my lovely wife
and return Eurydice.

Let us live on the Earth for a little while
and we'll hold death as our friend.
For sooner or later we'll return to you
as all mortals do in the end.

I beg you to let her come back to life,
King Dis and Queen Persephone,
but if you cannot grant my loving wish,
let me stay here in her company – for ever,
let me stay here in her company.

Orpheus sang, accompanying his words with the molten gold music of his lyre. Orpheus sang, and the bloodless spirits wept. The torments of the damned ceased while he sang. For the first time, we are told, the cheeks of the Furies, overcome by his music, were wet with tears. The king and queen of darkness could not refuse the singer. They called for Eurydice.

She had been with the new ghosts and came limping, because of her wounded foot. Orpheus took his bride by the hand. But he also took this warning from the king – Eurydice would follow him, but Orpheus must not look back until he left the Underworld.

The couple took the steep path through regions of utter silence, a rough track, hard to see and misty in the blackness. Upwards and upwards towards the light they walked. As they were reaching the rocky step into the brightness of the world, Orpheus, afraid that his bride might stumble and eager to see her in the light, looked back at her.

Instantly Eurydice slipped away down into the darkness. Orpheus stretched out his arms, trying to catch her or grip her hand. But his hands were full of empty air.

Dying for a second time, Eurydice did not reproach her husband. (She could only have complained that he loved her too much.) She said one last, soft "Farewell!" and then fell back into the land of ghosts.

Orpheus was driven mad by the double death of his beloved. He asked to cross the River Styx a second time. But the ferryman drove him away. For seven days he sat on that cold, grim riverbank, shivering in thin clothes and with nothing to eat.

Then he turned his back on the Underworld and went to live in the high mountains. Three years later he was still living there as a hermit. He had renounced the love of all women. But many of them fell in love with the great singer, and they were unhappy to be rejected.

Orpheus sat on a hill and played his lyre. It was a bare hill, with no kind of shade. But when he played, the trees gathered round to listen and shade was created. All the trees came – the oaks with their deep foliage, the soft linden, the beech, the laurel-tree, the brittle hazel, the ash which we use for making spears, the smooth silver birch, the bowing ilex, the pleasant plane, the slim tamarisk, the myrtle and many more. The light-footed ivy came, and the vines with their grapes, the mountain-ash, the tall pines, the arbutus and the lofty palm tree.

All the trees crowded round to hear him play. And the animals gathered there too – every animal you could name.

But, as he sang and charmed the trees, animals, birds and even the rocks, he was seen by a wild gang of women from Thrace. They wore the skins of wild beasts and tried to make up songs to the music of his lyre, screaming at the tops of their voices.

The musician did not even look at them.

Then one of them shouted, "There's the man who scorns us!" and threw her spear straight at the mouth of Orpheus. But the spear was made from one of the nearby trees and it refused to strike him, swerving away and only scratching his cheek.

Another threw a stone, but, even as it hurtled through the air, the stone was enchanted by the sweet voice and lyre, and dropped down at the singer's feet as if to ask forgiveness. But still the women attacked. They were mad with anger. All their weapons would have been useless under the spell of his song – but his music was swamped by the uproar of the drums, flutes, hand-clapping and screaming of these women, followers of the wine-god Bacchus.

The women tore apart many of the birds, snakes and animals which had gathered round to listen to Orpheus. Then they raised their blood-stained hands against him, turning on him like a flock of birds who find an owl wandering in the daylight. It was like watching a stag in the arena as the dogs close in on him. They pelted him with clods of earth, branches torn from trees, and sharp stones. They chased away a group of farm-workers and seized their hoes and spades for weapons. They hacked apart the cattle which stood in between them and the singer.

Then they set to work on Orpheus and struck him to the ground.

Through those lips, which once enchanted the rocks, the trees and all wild animals, he sang his last breath, and his soul flew away into the blue air.

All the birds wept for Orpheus, and the crowd of animals, and the stern rocks and the trees which had so often gathered round him. Yes, the trees shed their leaves in grief and the water-nymphs, who love bright colours, all wore black.

Parts of the poet's limbs lay scattered all around, but his head and his lyre fell into the river. While they floated in midstream the lyre produced some mournful chords, the dead tongue murmured and the banks of the river replied.

The head and the lyre were carried downstream and washed up on a beach. There a fierce snake appeared, its scales dripping with spray. It attacked the head. But Apollo, the father of Orpheus, appeared at the last moment and drove off the snake as it reared back to bite. He hardened and froze the snake into stone, just as it was, with deadly, yawning jaws.

The ghost of the singer hurried down under the Earth. He recognised all the dark places he had seen before. Searching through the fields of the blessed, he found Eurydice and took her in his eager arms. Here the lovers walk together side by side. Sometimes she walks ahead, sometimes he does – but now he can look safely back at his Eurydice.

But Bacchus did not allow the murder of Orpheus to go unpunished. Sad to lose the musician who played for his high ceremonies, the god gathered all the women who were present at the murder, and tied them up with roots.

As soon as they tried to walk, the ground clutched at their toes and dragged them down into the earth. Like birds with their claws caught in snares, who flap and flutter, but draw the trap tighter as they struggle – so these women tried to escape.

But the tough roots held. As they wondered where their fingers had gone, where were their feet? – they saw the bark come crawling up their legs. If they tried to slap their thighs in anger, they hit solid wood. Their soft breasts also turned to oak, and their arms and shoulders – solid oak. They had become trees – but now there was nobody to sing for them.

THE SCULPTOR'S PRIZE

Pygmalion was a wonderful artist, but he was lonely. None of the women in Cyprus, his island, seemed perfect enough to be his bride. So he lived by himself, unhappily, for many years.

But one day he carved the figure of a woman from snow-white ivory. He made it more beautiful than any woman ever born – so beautiful that he fell in love with his masterpiece.

Its face was the face of a real woman. You'd think she was alive and longing to breathe and move. Pygmalion gazed at her, admiring his own handiwork and on fire with love for her.

Over and over again he touched that body – was it flesh or ivory? He kissed the adorable statue and imagined his kisses were returned by those white lips.

He spoke to it in the warm, silly language of lovers. He embraced it and felt as if his fingers were sinking into its limbs. He stepped back suddenly, afraid he might leave bruises on that perfection.

He whispered to it, he brought it the kind of presents young women like – shells and bright pebbles, small birds and flowers of every colour, lilies and beads and amber necklaces.

He dressed it in soft robes, placed jewelled rings upon its fingers. He fitted it with pearl earrings and necklaces of gold. All of these were beautiful, but the statue was most beautiful when it wore nothing at all.

He laid it on a couch draped with purple silks, called it his darling, and propped its reclining head upon pillows filled with down – as if it could enjoy their softness.

The feast day of Venus arrived, and all Cyprus came to celebrate. Pure white heifers with gold-covered horns were sacrificed and incense floated heavenwards from the altars. Pygmalion made his offering to the goddess, then nervously prayed: "Dear gods, grant that I may marry" – he did not dare say "my statue" – "somebody just like my woman of ivory."

Golden Venus was there at her own festival, of course. She heard the sculptor's prayer and, to show she understood, made the flame on her altar blaze brightly and leap into the air three times.

Pygmalion hurried home and kissed his work of art as it lay upon the couch. The statue seemed warm. He kissed her again and touched her breast. The ivory softened under his hand and yielded to his fingers, like wax left out in the sunshine. He stepped back, astonished. Was it an illusion? He reached out and touched her again. Yes, she was alive! She was a real woman. He could feel the blood beating through her veins.

He sang his thanks to generous Venus. And then he kissed his woman's lips with his lips. She felt his kisses and blushed. Then she raised her head and her timid eyes saw the sky for the first time. And then she saw her lover, her creator.

Venus blessed this marriage, and within nine months a little girl was born to them. She was called Paphos – and there is an island named after her.

THE LOVE GODDESS IN LOVE

Once there was a myrtle tree in Arabia which gave birth to a fine baby boy. He grew to be Adonis, one of the most handsome young men in the world.

Cupid and his mother Venus were playing by the river. One of his love arrows accidentally scratched her breast. Laughing, she pushed her boy away. But the wound was more serious than she thought. When she looked up, she saw Adonis.

She was entranced by the young man's beauty. She forgot about her favourite islands. She even failed to visit her home in the skies – now she loved Adonis more than Heaven itself.

Venus had once spent her days lying on a mossy couch in the shade, becoming more beautiful every hour. But now she followed Adonis everywhere – over craggy mountains, through tangled woods, through stony thistle-beds and thorns – she strode across the land with her skirts tied up round her knees, like Diana the huntress. She cheered on the hounds and chased the hurdling hare, the quivering she-deer and the stag with his tall branches. But she avoided the violent wild boars, the slavering wolves, the iron-clawed bears and the slaughtering lions. She warned Adonis against such beasts – as if young men ever listen to warnings.

"Be brave when you're hunting timid creatures," she said. "But beware of savage beasts. Your youth and good looks, which I find so exciting, will only stir up the hunger of such monsters. The red-eyed boar is your worst enemy. He swoops down like a thunderstorm. His curving tusks strike like lightning. Avoid him at all costs."

"Of course," said Adonis, and he smiled.

Venus could not resist his smile. "Look," she said, "in the shade of this poplar tree there's a couch of soft grass. That's lucky. I would like to rest here with you." So she lay down on the ground and on him too. She used his chest for a pillow, and, punctuating her words with kisses, told him this story:

ATALANTA THE RUNNER

"Maybe you've heard of Atalanta the Runner – the young woman who outpaced all male athletes? She was raised by a she-bear – no wonder she could move so fast. Believe me, she was the best. And she was beautiful too. Atalanta went to the Oracle of Delphi to find out who she'd marry. This is how the god answered her:

"'Marriage is not for you. Run away from all husbands, yet you will not run away. Though you will live, you will lose yourself.' Terrified by this prophecy, she lived alone in the shadowy woods, and angrily refused her would-be lovers with these words:

"'I won't be won as a wife, until I'm beaten in a race. Run against me if you must. Win the race, and you win Atalanta. But if you lose, the prize is death. These are the rules.' Yes, she was merciless, but her beauty was so bewitching that even on these terms, plenty of fools rushed to compete.

"Now, young Hippomenes had taken his seat to be judge of the dangerous race. He made fun of the eager runners: 'Don't risk your life for any wife!'

"But then he saw Atalanta's face. And he saw her body as she strode, stripped down for the race, to the starting line. Her beauty was very like mine, Adonis, or like yours if you were a woman. Hippomenes was astonished and stretched out his hands and shouted, 'Forgive me, everyone, for making fun of you. I hadn't seen this wonderful prize.'

As he spoke, his heart caught fire. 'Why don't I try my luck?' he thought. 'The gods help those who help themselves.'

"At this moment Atalanta raced by him like a golden arrow. The way she ran gave her a special beauty. For the breeze caught and twirled the ribbons round her ankles. The curls of her hair flew above her white shoulders. Her thin dress rippled and over her fair body a pink colour spread, just like white marble in the rosy dawn. As Hippomenes watched, she passed the winning post.

"He crowned Atalanta with the winner's laurels.

"Then he looked deep into the eyes of the young woman and whispered, 'Why run against this mob of snails? Race against me. My father was the grandson of Neptune. I am a great-grandson of the king of the ocean. Beat me, and you'll be famous as the conqueror of Hippomenes.'

"Atalanta gazed at him and her eyes softened. She wanted to conquer him, but she wanted to be conquered. So she said, 'I am not worth the price. It's not your beauty that touches my heart – though it could touch me – but you are only a boy. On your way, stranger, No other maiden will refuse you. But why should I care for you, when I've let so many others die?

"If you die of love for me, everyone will hate me. Please don't race against me. If you do, I hope you prove the faster runner. Poor Hippomenes, I wish you'd never seen me! You really deserve to live. If I were only a luckier lady – you are the only one I'd want to marry.'

"That is what she said, in her innocence. For she had never been in love. Now she felt the first flames of passion, but she did not understand their burning.

"The people stood up and shouted, demanding another race. It was then that Hippomenes, the great-grandson of Neptune, called to me: 'Beautiful Venus, please help me in this race, and feed the flames of love which you have lit.' A kindly breeze carried this charming prayer up to me. It moved my heart.

"Time was short. There is a bright orchard in Cyprus, dedicated to me. In it stands a tree gleaming with golden leaves. Its bark crackles with the same gold. I had just visited that tree and happened to have in my hand three of its golden apples. Invisible to everybody except Hippomenes, I taught him how he must use this magical fruit.

"The trumpets sounded for the race. Atalanta and Hippomenes stood side by side, staring straight ahead. Then the two of them, crouched low, flashed from their places and skimmed over the sandy track with flying feet. They seemed capable of sprinting across the ocean with dry feet or speeding over the top of golden fields of standing wheat. The young man was urged on by the crowd: 'Get on with it, Hippomenes! Go! Now – use everything! Don't slow down: you've got to win!'

"He was glad to hear them – but so was she. Often, when she could have overtaken him, she paused and gazed into his face, leaving him behind only reluctantly. He was panting now – short, dry breaths – and the winning post was a long way off. At last he deliberately dropped one of the three golden apples.

"Atalanta, amazed, saw it fall. She turned back to pick up the shining globe. Hippomenes passed her. The spectators roared. She put on a burst of speed, catching up with the youth, then leaving him standing.

"Again she stopped as the second apple fell. She fumbled, picked it up – then followed and overtook her rival.

"They were on the home stretch. 'Now help me, Venus, for you gave me this!' he shouted, and threw the last shining gold apple with all his strength into the far corner of a field. Atalanta didn't know whether to chase it or not. I made up her mind for her. I also quadrupled the weight of the last apple, giving her an extra handicap. And, to cut a long race short, the young woman was overtaken. Hippomenes had won. The victor led away his beautiful prize.

"Don't you think, Adonis, that he should have thanked me? But his mind was on other things. He didn't even burn me a few sticks of incense. And I do so love the smell of incense. I was suddenly very angry, being slighted like that. I made up my mind never to be rejected again. I would make an example of them both.

"They were passing a temple hidden in the woods. They had travelled a long way and decided to rest. Hippomenes, prompted by me, was full of passion. He led the way into a cave where an old priest had set images of the ancient gods. Hippomenes defiled this place with his lust. The wooden statues turned away their eyes.

"But he and his bride were punished by the mother of the gods. The lovers changed in mid-embrace. Their smooth necks grew rough with tawny manes. Their fingers curved and hardened into claws. Their arms became padded legs. Their chests swelled with shield-shaped breastbones. Their tasselled tails swept along the sandy ground. Their faces became harsh and hairy. They could only speak by growling. And for their honeymoon they haunted the wild woods – two lions, slaves to the mother of the gods.

"Adonis, please avoid savage beasts like these – and all other wild animals which turn to face you and fight. Avoid them, sweet boy, or your manly courage will wreck our happiness."

Venus had warned him. Then off she flew, drawn by her silver swans across the heavens. But the young man's courage wouldn't let him take her good advice.

By chance, his hounds flushed a wild boar from his hiding place. As it charged out of the woods, Adonis threw his spear and pierced its flank. The boar used his snout to uproot the spear, wet with blood, from his side. Then he turned, lowered his great tusks and charged.

Adonis ran for his life – but not fast enough.

The boar sank a long tusk deep into the young man's groin, and threw him on the sand, where he lay, dying, beside a glassy waterfall and a calm turquoise pool.

From her swan chariot high up in the air, Venus heard the moaning of the dying Adonis. She turned her silver swans back towards him. When she looked down he was lying there, lifeless and soaked in blood. She dived from her chariot and clung to him.

"This is the work of the Fates," she said, "But they shan't have the last word. Adonis, my love for you will always be remembered. Each year a flower shall act out your death.

She sprinkled the blood of Adonis with the sweet-smelling nectar of the gods. The blood and nectar mingled and fizzed, as when clear bubbles rise up from the yellow mud at the bottom of a pond.

One hour later a flower sprang up. It was the colour of a young man's blood. This is the anemone. It reminds us of all those who die young.

Every year in spring, when the streams turn red as the snow melts and red earth slides down the mountain, the anemone returns. But the flower does not live for long. The winds shake off its lightly-clinging petals, which fall all too soon. This is why many people call it the wind-flower.

PURPLE HAIR

In his shining palace, high above the blue-green sea, lived Nisus, King of Megara. He was an old man now, feared and respected, for there was something magical about King Nisus. His head was crowned with fine, silver hair, with one glowing lock of purple. This magical tress contained the safety of the king and of his kingdom.

Megara was at war. Its walls were under siege by Minos, King of Crete, trying to avenge the murder of his son. The siege had lasted six months, with hundreds of deaths on each side. Still nobody knew if the city would fall.

Nisus had a young daughter called Scylla. In peacetime she loved to climb up the highest turret of the palace and spin little pebbles through the air so that they rolled and bounced down the stone walls, making a bright, clinking music as they tumbled.

Now it was wartime, she still climbed up to her perch. From it she watched the battling armies. As the war dragged on, she came to know the names of the Cretan chieftains. She could tell them apart by their robes, their weapons and their horses.

Her favourite in the enemy army was its commander, King Minos, son of Europa. She admired the way he wore his great plumed helmet. If he carried his golden shield, that made him even more handsome. When he hurled his spear, she gasped at the strength of his muscles. When he drew his wide bow, she held her breath in delight.

But when he took off his helmet and showed his face, or wore a purple cloak and rode his milk-white charger, Scylla screamed out loud. She wished she could be the sword he held or the reins he gathered in his hand. If only she could leap from her tower down into the Cretan camp and open the bronze gates of her city to the enemy, or do something else to please King Minos!

The daydreaming princess sat, gazing at the white tents of Crete and said to herself, "I don't know whether to laugh or cry about this awful war. I'm in love with Minos and he's my enemy. Suppose he took me hostage. Then I could be with him. I would be a promise of peace. But I'd never

betray my own city. No. All the same, many towns have done better after being conquered, so long as the victorious general is merciful.

"I think Minos is fighting what they call a just war, to avenge his murdered son. And his army's as strong as his cause. It looks as if Megara will be defeated anyway. And if that's our fate, why should his fist of iron unbar our gates, rather than my loving hands?

"There'll be far less bloodshed if I give myself up and end the war now. But my father holds the keys of the city. He's all that stands in my way. I wish to God I had no father!

"All I need is that lock of hair – that lock more precious than any gold – that purple lock on my father's head – that will grant me all my wishes."

By now it was dark. The palace was asleep. Scylla tiptoed into her father's bedroom, a pair of shears in her hand. Carefully she cut off the magical purple lock. She walked out of the room, out of the palace. Holding high the purple lock, she walked past the guards, out of the city, through the hypnotised ranks of the Cretan army and up to Minos as he sat on his throne.

"I have done what I have done in the name of love," she said. "I am Scylla, daughter of King Nisus. Now I offer you my home and my city. Take me to Crete with you. I ask for no reward except your heart. Let this famous lock of purple hair prove that I love you, for it is not just a hank of hair – it is my father's life."

Scylla held out the purple hair to Minos.

The king clasped his hands to his forehead in horror. He was silent for a time. Then he spoke, stonily:

"For what you have done, may the gods banish you from the world of men and women. May you be exiled from the land and the sea. No traitor like you shall ever visit Crete, my holy island, where Jove himself spent his childhood days."

Then Minos, who believed in justice, imposed fair terms on the defeated city of Megara. He ordered his army back to their ships. The ships set sail and sped home towards Crete.

When Scylla saw them leaving she was mad with anger. She yelled insults at Minos, she howled complaints about her banishment from the land and the sea and from the kingdom of Crete. She kept her eyes fixed on the ship of King Minos and she screamed so desperately that her throat began to tear itself. "It's no good! I'm going to follow you! Wherever you sail, I'll always be with you!"

She dived into the water and swam ferociously, until she reached the ship of King Minos. She reached up and clung on to its stern, hated and unwelcome.

But her father, without his purple lock to guard him, had been changed into an osprey with tawny wings. As he hovered in the sky, he saw his daughter, then dived to tear her with his hooked beak as she hung on to the Cretan craft.

Terrified, she let go, but as she fell, a breeze seemed to carry her upwards and over the sea. Her hands had sprouted feathers and her arms were wings. Changed to a bird, she is called 'shearwater', because she took shears to steal her father's purple lock of hair.

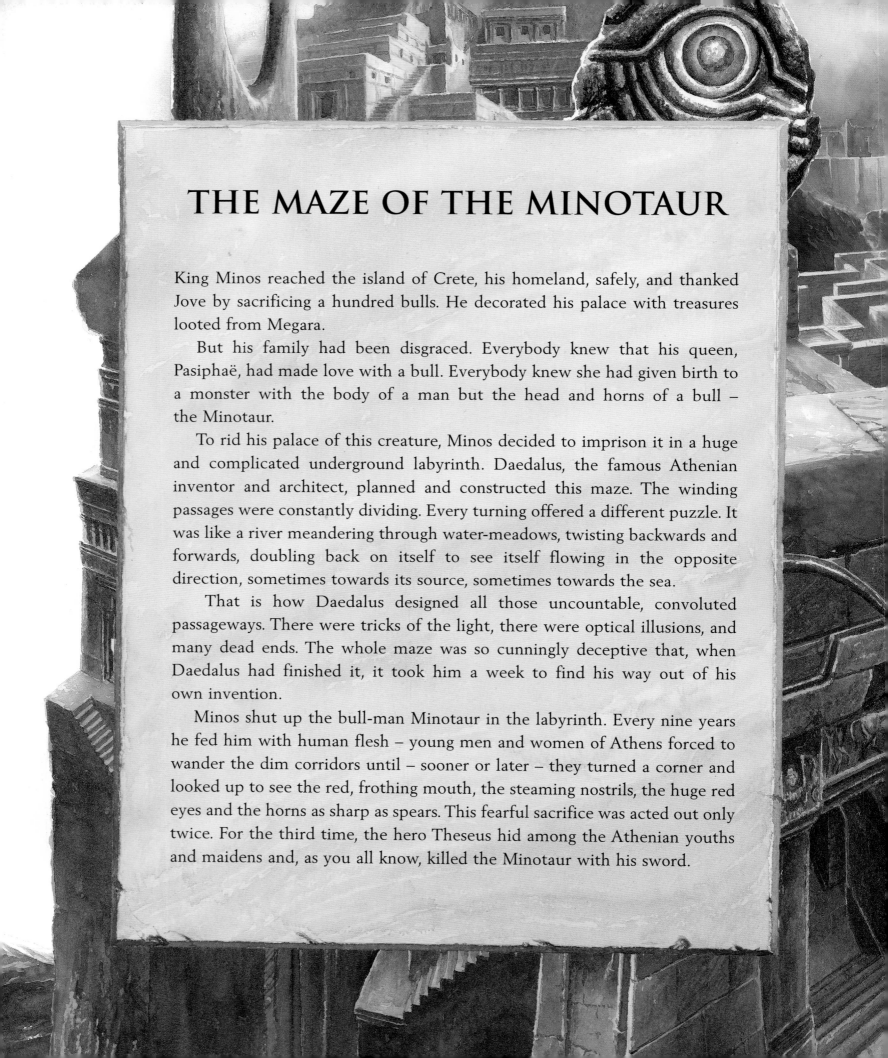

THE MAZE OF THE MINOTAUR

King Minos reached the island of Crete, his homeland, safely, and thanked Jove by sacrificing a hundred bulls. He decorated his palace with treasures looted from Megara.

But his family had been disgraced. Everybody knew that his queen, Pasiphaë, had made love with a bull. Everybody knew she had given birth to a monster with the body of a man but the head and horns of a bull – the Minotaur.

To rid his palace of this creature, Minos decided to imprison it in a huge and complicated underground labyrinth. Daedalus, the famous Athenian inventor and architect, planned and constructed this maze. The winding passages were constantly dividing. Every turning offered a different puzzle. It was like a river meandering through water-meadows, twisting backwards and forwards, doubling back on itself to see itself flowing in the opposite direction, sometimes towards its source, sometimes towards the sea.

That is how Daedalus designed all those uncountable, convoluted passageways. There were tricks of the light, there were optical illusions, and many dead ends. The whole maze was so cunningly deceptive that, when Daedalus had finished it, it took him a week to find his way out of his own invention.

Minos shut up the bull-man Minotaur in the labyrinth. Every nine years he fed him with human flesh – young men and women of Athens forced to wander the dim corridors until – sooner or later – they turned a corner and looked up to see the red, frothing mouth, the steaming nostrils, the huge red eyes and the horns as sharp as spears. This fearful sacrifice was acted out only twice. For the third time, the hero Theseus hid among the Athenian youths and maidens and, as you all know, killed the Minotaur with his sword.

How did Theseus escape from the labyrinth? The daughter of Minos, Ariadne, fell in love with him. She showed him how to unwind a spool of thread behind him and find his way out of the maze by following it.

Ariadne sailed with Theseus as far as the island of Naxos. There, like the ungrateful hero that he was, Theseus abandoned her. (He probably muttered that she had betrayed Minos, her father, and would sooner or later betray her lover, Theseus.)

But, as we know, Naxos is the favourite island of the wine-god. Ariadne was welcomed and comforted by the kindly Bacchus. So that she might shine for ever among the stars, he hurled her crown to the top of the night skies. It whirled up through the thin air. As it flew, its jewels were transformed into glittering fires.

You can still see the shape of that crown in the night sky, a fiery constellation between Hercules and the Serpent-Carrier.

ICARUS FALLS

For many years the inventor Daedalus lived in exile in Crete, because of a scandal which will be explained later in this story. But Daedalus longed to return to the great city of Athens. Meanwhile, King Minos pestered him with orders and ideas for elaborate weapons and war-engines. Escape seemed impossible – it's too far to swim from the island of Crete to the mainland. Even if Daedalus made a boat, the seas were infested by pirates. And even if he reached the shore, the roads to Athens seethed with robbers, soldiers and bandits of all kinds.

"At least the skies are free and open," thought the inventor. "That's how I'll travel. Minos may rule the land and sea – he has no power over the sky."

So he sat down at his desk and began to draw. By the time he stood up again, he had changed the laws of nature. Collecting feathers of all kinds, he laid them in rows, beginning with the smallest, next the middle-sized and finally the long ones. It's an arrangement rather like Pan-pipes, with each reed longer than the one before, forming a gentle slope.

Next he bound the middle and the lower side with twine and wax. Then he bent them into a gradual curve so that they imitated the wings of a great bird.

His son, Icarus, stood watching him. He laughed as he clutched at the feathers swirling round the workshop in the breeze, moulded little animals out of the yellow wax, and generally got in his father's way.

Finally the work was finished. The great inventor balanced his body between two of the wings and hovered in mid-air. Patiently, he taught his son to do the same and said, "Let me warn you, Icarus – fly through the middle air. Sink too low, the waves may soak your wings and weigh you down. Soar too high and the heat may burn them. Fly halfway between the heights and depths. And don't start gazing at the stars, trying to navigate by the Great Bear, the Wagoner or Orion with his sword. Just follow me."

While he explained to his son the rules of flying, Daedalus fastened the strange new wings on the boy's shoulders. As he worked and talked, the old craftsman's cheeks were wet with tears and his hands trembled. He kissed his son for the last time, and, rising on his own pair of wings, flew rapidly. He worried about his son like any bird who leads her unfledged youngster out of a high, safe nest into the dangerous air. He called out to his boy to come on – flapping his wings to show him how. Icarus responded with his own strong-beating wings.

A fisherman on the shore far below, clasping his bending rod, spots them and his mouth falls open like a carp's. A shepherd, leaning on his crook, looks up and whistles as his dog barks disbelievingly. A ploughman stops in mid-furrow and stands stock-still, his eyes like plums – these flying figures must be gods.

Father and son glided over the famous islands – leaving Delos and Paros behind them, passing Samos, the sacred island of Juno, Lebinthos and the honey island of Calymne.

Now Icarus began to enjoy the thrill of flying. Longing to ride up the open sky, he left his father way behind as he mounted higher and higher, scattering flocks of clouds as he rose – too high.

As Icarus flew close to the sun, its fierce rays scorched and softened the wax of his wings. The wax melted, the feathers flew away. He beat his strong arms up and down, but those arms were featherless, useless.

He called out his father's name until the last moment, as he drowned in the dark blue sea which is now named after him.

His frantic father, now no longer a father, shouted back, "Icarus, Icarus, where shall I find you?"

And then he saw the last of the falling feathers. And he saw his son's wings on the water. And he cursed his own cleverness and craft. He buried his boy's body in a rocky grave on the island we now call Icaria.

While Daedalus was burying his son, a chattering partridge watched him from a muddy ditch, flapped her wings and squawked happily. There'd never been a bird like this before – it was a living reminder of a death, of the scandal which had led to the inventor's exile from his beloved Athens.

His sister had asked him to educate her son Perdix, a lad of twelve, quick-witted and highly inventive. The boy spent the whole of one day examining the backbone of a fish. Next morning, using that backbone as a model, he cut a row of teeth in an iron blade and invented the first saw.

Perdix was also the first to attach one rod of iron to another with a joint, so that one stood still while the other turned, and, with a pen attached, could draw a circle.

But Daedalus grew jealous. This pupil seemed fated to surpass his master. So Daedalus took Perdix to visit the Acropolis. Hot sunshine. Perdix said something clever. Sudden rage. The master threw his pupil headfirst over the cliff. It didn't take a moment. (He claimed later that the boy tripped and fell.)

But Perdix didn't die. Minerva, Goddess of Wisdom, for whom the Acropolis was built, was watching. Minerva, who loves the talented, caught the falling boy, changed him into a bird and covered him with feathers in mid-fall.

His quickness went into his wings and legs, but he kept the name Perdix, which means "partridge". Even today, this bird never flies high and never builds her nests in tree-tops or on tall rocks. She flutters low along the ground and, remembering that terrible fall, is always scared of heights.

THE GOLDEN TOUCH

I want to sing about King Midas.
He was a little too much.
I'll tell you all about Midas
and the Golden Touch.

Bacchus said to Midas,
"Tell me, what would please your soul?"
Midas said, "I want the special touch
that turns everything to gold."

Bacchus said, "You've got it."
Midas said, "That's great!"
Then he picked up a broken-down wooden chair
and a battered old tin plate.

The chair was suddenly a golden throne
and the plate was golden too,
and Midas realised that his wish
for the Touch had really come true.

Yes, Midas got the Golden Touch.

Midas in the rose garden
brushed up against one petal –
all the roses turned to gold
and they smelled of rusty metal.

Then Midas felt like a little snack
and that was really tough,
for when he touched a juicy steak,
it turned to the yellow stuff.

Yes, Midas got the Golden Touch.

The king felt dry and thirsty
but, much to his disgust,
when he tried to swallow his favourite wine
it turned to golden dust.

Midas called to his loving queen –
didn't mean any harm,
but she turned to a golden statue
as soon as he touched her arm.

Yes, Midas got the Golden Touch.

"Bacchus!" shouted Midas,
"Tell me what to do!
Looks like I'm going to die of gold
because of this gift from you."

"Midas," Bacchus answered,
"You had better go
to my waterfall in the mountains
running cold as mountain snow.

"Better take your queen along with you,
and wash yourselves so much
that you wash away your crazy wish
and the curse of the Golden Touch."

Yes, Midas had the Golden Touch.

So they stood in the tumbling water
and they scrubbed themselves so much
that King Midas washed away his wish
and he lost the Golden Touch.

Yes, Midas lost the Golden Touch.

THE SONG CONTEST

So Midas escaped from death by gold. Now he hated wealth. He abandoned his treasures and his glorious palace and ran away to live in the hills. There he worshipped the god Pan, who lived in a mountain cave.

This spectacular cave had many tunnels, some running downwards into the darkness, some upwards towards the light. Its main cavern was a great hall with a high ceiling and stalactites and stalagmites like multi-coloured pillars. The wide floor of red clay contained a deep, clear pool which gave a still and perfect reflection.

The mountain-nymphs loved to sit around the pool, not just looking at themselves, but also listening to the songs sung by Pan and the airy tunes he played on his pipes.

"Your songs are wonderful," they said, and Pan agreed. "Sing us another," said Midas, who was visiting.

Pan sang a new song, then played a tune whose sweet notes chased each other through the echoes of the high cavern. He laid down his pipes. "I don't think even Apollo, the god of music, could play that well, do you?" asked Pan.

"Of course not, Pan," chorused the nymphs, but they jumped when a golden voice resounded through the cave.

"Pan, you flatter yourself. I, Phoebus Apollo, challenge you to a musical duel. Let the local mountain, Tmolus, be the judge. A mountain cannot be bribed or swayed by friendship."

The mountain announced, in a hoarse and stony whisper, that he would judge the contest. He shook his ears free from shrubs and gorse. He wore a wreath of oak-leaves on his stormy-coloured hair. Acorns hung on his forehead and around his shoulders was gathered a scarf of softest clouds.

Tmolus turned his great summit towards Pan, the god of shepherds, and said, "Your judge is ready."

Pan played upon his pipes a thousand shimmering silver notes which amazed everyone, particularly King Midas, who whispered to the nearest nymph, "Enchanting, quite enchanting."

Then Tmolus turned his mighty rock face towards Apollo: "Apollo, may we hear your song?"

On his golden head Phoebus Apollo wore a wreath of laurels from Parnassus. His purple cloak swept along the ground as he strode to the singing place. In his left hand he held his lyre, inlaid with jewels and ivory. In his right hand he held the plectrum. From the way he stood, you knew he was an artist.

Then he began to pluck sweet music from the strings and raised his pure gold voice in song until everybody in the cave was overwhelmed by his artistry – all except one.

The mountain judge nodded to Apollo and told Pan that he must lower his pipes in homage to the lyre. Pan obeyed with a smile.

"That's not fair!" cried the harsh voice of Midas, "Pan was much better. Now, I know you'll all say that I don't know how to sing and play music, but you don't have to be a horse to judge a race, do you? I may not be a scholar, but I know a good tune when I hear one. Pan's the winner!"

Everyone stared at his cloth-eared stupidity. Apollo gave a magical wave of his hand. The dull ears of Midas began to lengthen and fill up with shaggy, grey hair. They twitched and flopped around. The rest of Midas remained human, but when he looked into the cave's dark pool, he saw he had the ears of an ass. With a desperate bray, he galloped out of the cave, followed by the laughter of the mountain-nymphs.

He avoided being seen by any humans until he had found a length of scarlet cloth and wrapped it round his forehead and tall ears like a turban with two points. It looked odd, but nobody could guess what lay underneath.

Only the slave who cut his hair, and was sworn to secrecy on pain of death, knew about his donkey ears. Of course, this slave was bursting to tell the king's secret. Finally he ran into a water-meadow beside the road to Athens and dug a hole in the ground with his hand. He muttered the secret into the hole: "King Midas has the ears of an ass!" Then he filled the hole with earth and mud and ran home.

But a thick bed of water-reeds began to grow over that spot, and at the year's end they were fully grown, and, stirring in the gentle breeze, they whispered to every passer-by, "King Midas has the ears of an ass!"

So now the whole world knows.

THE PROUD WEAVER

Remember Arachne. She was a weaver and she was a wonder. Her mother was a quiet woman, who died while Arachne was a little girl. Her father was ordinary enough, except that his arms were often purple through dyeing wool for his daughter

Arachne became famous for her artistry. Often the mountain-nymphs left their vineyards and the water-nymphs abandoned their rivers to crowd into her bright weaving-room. It was a joy to watch her working. She had such a light touch that her hands seemed to dance:

Winding the raw wool into a ball
or shaping the fleece with her fingertips,
reaching backwards to the distaff
for more wool, light as cloud-fleece,
drawing it out into long soft threads
or twisting the spindle with her clever thumb
or setting her needle flashing
to create a picture in front of your eyes...
A wood-nymph gasped and said,
"You must have been taught by
the goddess of art – Minerva herself."

But Arachne laughed at such talk. She said, "I never had a teacher. I taught myself. If Minerva's so wonderful, let her come and weave a better tapestry than mine. If she can do that, I'll pay any kind of forfeit."

Being a goddess, Minerva heard this impertinent challenge. Instantly she disguised herself as an old woman, stuck an old grey wig on her head and, leaning on a crooked stick, tottered into Arachne's workroom. Arachne glanced at her and said, "Off you go – I'm too busy for beggars."

"I don't beg for anything, young lady, I offer golden advice. Inspiration is all very well, but an artist needs experience. Listen – seek fame as a weaver. But grant first place to the goddess of art. Apologise for your boastful words. Pray humbly enough, and she'll have mercy on you."

But Arachne was a proud artist. She stared at the old woman with cold black eyes. She dropped the threads she was working with, stood up beside her loom and hissed angrily into the face of the disguised Minerva:

"You're old, you're daft and you've lived too long. Go bleat to your own daughter, if you have one. Let your precious goddess come and speak for herself. Or is she too scared to take me on?"

That did it. With one cry – "The goddess is here!" – Minerva threw off her disguise, and stood there in all her glory. The nymphs and local women bowed down to her. Only Arachne showed no fear. But she did blush, for a moment – a pink blush like dawn on a dangerous day for shepherds.

Still she wouldn't withdraw her challenge. She was excited by the idea of the competition and drunk with a dream of victory. Minerva didn't warn her again – she nodded once.

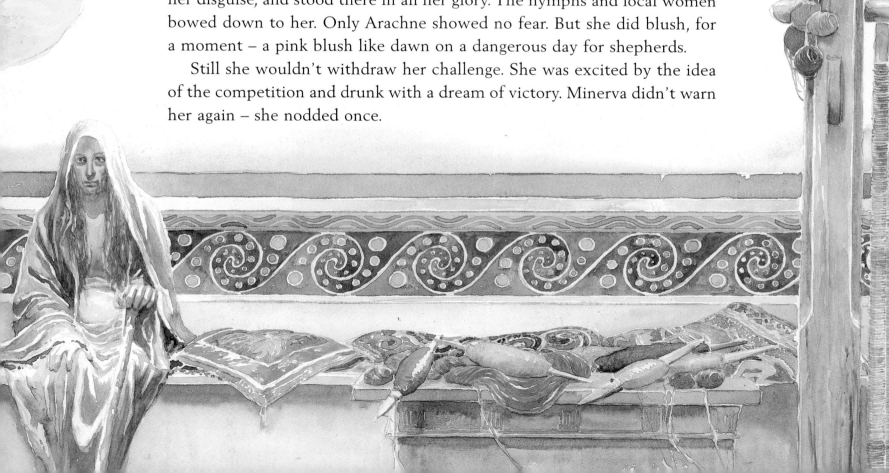

The contest is on.
The room is silent. Everyone's watching.
Two looms are set up at opposite ends of the weaving room.
The weavers begin.
They stretch the fine warp,
they bind the web upon the beam.
A tall rod separates the threads of the warp.
The woof is threaded through the warp
by sharp shuttles thrown by their cunning fingers.
As the woof shoots through, it is pressed into place
by the teeth of the long comb.
They both work speedily,
dresses fastened tight below their breasts.
Their clever hands move back and forth
as if dancing to silent music.
It's hard work, but it's joyful work
creating beauty.

They weave into their tapestries purple threads,
many colours changing gradually
from dark to bright.
It's like the sun striking through a rainstorm

and a rainbow's flying arch painting the sky
and, though a thousand colours dance
on the blue background, your eye can't make out
where one colour changes into another.
They weave in threads of gold
and on each loom grow many pictures based
on the good old stories.

This is what Minerva's tapestry shows:

The rock of Mars at the Acropolis
and the great argument about the naming of Athens.
There sit twelve mighty gods upon their thrones,
all of them easily recognisable:
Jove in his unmatched majesty –
calm, wise, benevolent and golden.

Neptune is shown striking the cliff
with his oceanic trident
so that a tidal wave of salty water gushes out –
his way of claiming the city
and saying, "It shall be named after me."

Minerva, whom the Greeks called Athene,
shows herself with her famous shield,
her helmet and her breastplate.
She stabs the earth with her sharp spear –
an olive tree springs up, laden with fruit.
The gods look on in wonder –
Minerva has defeated Neptune.
The city is named after her – Athens.

Minerva's tapestry is dignified,
majestic and commanding.
It shows the greatness of the gods
so powerfully, you go weak at the knees
with admiration.

Then, so her rival may understand
how the gods repay impertinence,
she weaves into the corners of the web
four pictures telling the sad stories
of those who challenged the gods and lost.

The first shows two giants who defied the gods
and were turned into bleak grey mountains.

The second shows the Queen of the Pygmies,
whom Juno magicked into a crane
and forced to make war on her own people.

The third shows how Antigone
dared insult Juno, and was transmogrified
into a stork with snowy feathers
and a long, clapping bill.

The fourth shows Cinyras mourning for his daughters
who were frozen into the marble steps of a temple.

Finally Minerva weaves, all around her work,
a border of olive leaves, which speak of peace.
The tapestry's finished – with her beloved olive tree
the goddess signs her work.

This is what Arachne's tapestry shows:

Here's Europa, a pretty girl at the seaside
seduced by Jove disguised as a bull.
With his rolling eyes and hot-cloud breath
you can almost smell the rampaging bull
and the salt of the crashing waves.
The open-mouthed girl stares back to the land,
yelling to her friends
to save her from the monster.

Far above the high-leaping waves
she weaves the struggling girl Asterië
carried off by Jove, in the shape of an eagle,
to his nest in the mountains.

She shows Leda lying, paralysed,
under the beating wings of the swan
whose real name is Jove.

She shows how Antiope had twins
after Jove tricked her, disguised as a satyr.
She demonstrates many more
of the great god's stratagems:
how he became Amphitryon to seduce Alcmena,
a shower of gold to make love to Danaë,
and many other cunning disguises –
a flame, a shepherd and a spotted snake.
Very amusing for the father of the gods,
less so for the mortal women he rapes.

She shows Neptune too, in his disguises
for tricking and seducing mortals:
Neptune the bull, the ram, the horse,
the bird and the smiling dolphin.
All of these are shown
at the scenes of his adventures.

She shows Apollo dressed like a peasant,
also wearing a hawk's feathers
and draped in a lion's skin.
She shows how Bacchus fooled Erigone
with a trick bunch of grapes,
and how Saturn, in the shape of a horse,
became the father of Chiron the centaur.

That's how Arachne sees these gods –
cold-hearted tricksters and wild rapists,
with no love in their hearts.
They seem like giant children –
sometimes frightening, sometimes silly.

The humans in her stories
are imperfect men and women –
so simple and so complicated
and beautiful and different from each other
that you fall in love with each of them in turn.

But all her woven pictures glow
with passion, humour and intelligence.
The gods, humans and animals she shows
are so alive, they take your breath away
and the landscapes they inhabit
are so lovely that you laugh and weep at the same time.

Arachne decorates the edge of her tapestry
with intertwining wild flowers and ivy.

In all of Arachne's work
Minerva can find no artistic fault.
Maddened by her rival's supremacy
the golden-haired goddess
spits on Arachne's tapestry
with its blasphemous account
of the great gods,
then, with her long, sharp fingernails,
tears and rips the work
into shreds and threads and specks of coloured dust.

Next, she takes up her heavy boxwood shuttle
and smashes it three times, four times,
on Arachne's head.
Unable to take any more, the girl
pulls a noose round her own neck.
Minerva compassionately raises her up
and says, "Oh no, you have to live.
You must live and hang as well, proud girl,
and the same punishment I give you now
will pass to your descendants."

As Minerva turns to go, she sprinkles Arachne
with juice of magic herbs – at once
the young woman's hair falls out,
then her nose and ears vanish.
Her head shrinks to the size of a raisin.
Her body becomes small and shapeless.
Those slender skilful fingers
are needle-thin legs stuck around her sides.
All the rest is belly.

And from this belly
she spins a fine thread;
she has become an ordinary spider.
Only silly people are scared of such spiders.
Only bad-tempered and jealous people
hit spiders with heavy objects.

Arachne the spider keeps on spinning,
creating the most delicate webs in the world.

She was the most skilful weaver of them all.
Artists – remember Arachne.

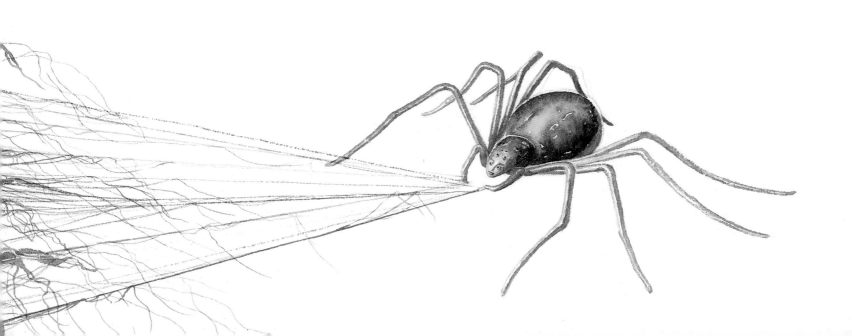

GOODBYE

I have shown these stories to my friends
and some of them say:

"These gods are cunning, compassionate,
callous, childish, creative and cruel by turns.
They're passionate, proud and petty."

But me, I don't say that.
What I say is this:
read my stories again and –
be careful what you say about the gods.

Now my work's done, and nothing can destroy it –
not lightning, sword or fire shall tear its pages,
nor shall they drown in the swamp of the ages.
Now my work's done, let everyone enjoy it.

When my life's done, let the best part of me
be carried swiftly to a far meadow
beyond the furthest star
to live in immortality.

Throughout the lands conquered in war
by mighty Rome, my words will live
while people love them, and so give
this book a life for ever more.

THE OLD GODS

The Ancient Roman name for the god or goddess is shown first, followed by the earlier, Ancient Greek name in brackets.

AEOLUS (Aeolus) – God of the winds

Phoebus APOLLO (Apollo) – God of the sun, music, poetry and healing

BACCHUS (Dionysus) – God of wine

CERES (Demeter) – Goddess of corn, fruit and crops

CUPID (Eros) – boy God of love

DIANA (Artemis) – virgin Goddess of the moon, hunting and fertility

FURIES (Erinnyes) – The Furies

IRIS (Iris) – Goddess of the rainbow, messenger of the gods

JOVE or Jupiter (Zeus) – Supreme god and lord of Heaven

JUNO (Hera) – Queen of Heaven and goddess of marriage and women

MARS (Ares) – God of war

MERCURY (Hermes) – Messenger god and god of science and commerce

MINERVA (Pallas Athene) – Goddess of wisdom, the arts and trade

MORPHEUS (Morpheus) – God of dreams

NEPTUNE (Poseidon) – God of the sea. (Also Nereus and Oceanus)

PROSERPINA (Persephone) – Goddess of the Underworld

SATURN – Father of the gods. God of seed-time and harvest

THEMIS – Goddess of justice

VENUS (Aphrodite) – Goddess of love and beauty

VERTUMNUS – God of the seasons

VULCAN (Hephaestus) – God of fire and blacksmiths

A NOTE ON OVID

Publius Ovidius Naso (43 BC – 17 AD) was born into a distinguished family and educated in Rome. His books the *Amores* and the *Ars Amatoria* achieved enormous success; he also wrote the *Heroides* and the *Fasti*. But most people remember him for the *Metamorphoses*, which he never completed. In 8 AD, accused of high treason, he was banished to the Black Sea coast, where he died in exile.

HOW TO PRONOUNCE
THE GREEK NAMES

Acoetes (A-KOI-tees)

Actaeon (Ak-TAY-on)

Aeolus (EE-o-lus)

Alcmena (Alk-MAY-na)

Amphitryon (Am-FIT-tree-on)

Antigone (An-TIG-on-ee)

Antiope (An-TY-o-pee)

Arachne (A-RACK-nee)

Ariadne (A-ree-AD-nee)

Asterië (As-TE-ree-eh)

Athene (Ath-EE-nee)

Baucis (BOUGH-kiss)

Callisto (Ka-LIS-toh)

Calymne (Ka-LIM-nee)

Cenyras (KEN-i-ras)

Cerberus (SER-ber-us)

Ceres (SEER-ees)

Chiron (KEER-on)

Cyane (SY-a-nee)

Cycnus (SIK-nus)

Daedalus (DEE-da-lus)

Danaë (DAN-ah-ee)

Deucalion (DEW-kay-lee-on)

Epaphus (EP-a-fus)

Erigone (E-RIG-on-ee)

Erysichthon (E-ri-SIK-thon)

Eurydice (Yew-RI-di-see)

Hesperi (HES-per-ee)

Hippomenes (Hi-POM-en-ees)

Icarus (IK-a-rus)

Io (EYE-oh)

Leda (LAY-da)

Lycaon (Li-KAY-on)

Metamorphoses (Me-ta-MOR-foh-sees)

Midas (MY-das)

Minos (MY-nos)

Minotaur (MY-no-tor)

Morpheus (MORF-yus)

Nemesis (NE-me-sis)

Neptune (NEP-tewn)

Pasiphaë (Pa-SIF-ah-ee)

Peneus (PEN-yus)

Persephone (Per-SEF-on-ee)

Phaethon (FAY-thon)

Philemon (Fi-LAY-mon)

Phoebus (FEE-bus)

Phrygia (FRIJ-ya)

Pirithous (Pi-RITH-oh-us)

Pygmalion (Pig-MAY-li-on)

Pyrrha (PI-ra)

Styx (STIX)

Syrinx (SI-rinx)

Taenarus (Ten-AH-rus)

Themis (THEM-is)

Tmolus (TMOH-lus)

Typhon (TY-fon)

Tyresias (Ty-REE-see-as)